"You tell me I don't know what I'm doing. Yet every instinct tells me having you in my arms is the right thing... Have I kissed you before?"

Jacinta felt her cheeks flame. "Yes."

"Have we made love?"

The answer stuck in her throat. "Mathiaz, please..."

"Answer the question or you're fired."

She hesitated, wondering whether to call his bluff. "Go ahead and fire me," she said quietly. The thought of leaving swamped her in misery, but anything was better than dealing with this. Mathiaz couldn't know that he was rubbing salt into a raw wound with every word.

"I wish I could. But as long as you hold the key to the hole in my memory, I'm not letting you go," he said.

His eyes brightened, boring into her. "I need you, Jacinta. To help me remember."

Dear Reader,

Grab a front-row seat on the roller-coaster ride of falling in love. This month, Silhouette Romance offers heart-spinning thrills, including the latest must-read from THE COLTONS saga, a new enchanting SOULMATES title and even a sexy Santa!

Become a fan—if you aren't hooked already!—of THE COLTONS with the newest addition to the legendary family saga, Teresa Southwick's *Sky Full of Promise* (#1624), about a stone-hearted doctor in search of a temporary fiancée. And single men don't stay so for long in Jodi O'Donnell's BRIDGEWATER BACHELORS series. The next rugged Texan loses his solo status in *His Best Friend's Bride* (#1625).

Love is magical, and it's especially true in our wonderful SOULMATES series, which brings couples together in extraordinary ways. In DeAnna Talcott's *Her Last Chance* (#1628), virgin heiress Mallory Chevalle travels thousands of miles in search of a mythical horse—and finds her destiny in the arms of a stubborn, but irresistible rancher. And a case of amnesia reunites past lovers—but the heroine's painful secret could destroy her second chance at happiness, in Valerie Parv's *The Baron & the Bodyguard*, the latest exciting installment in THE CARRAMER LEGACY.

To get into the holiday spirit, enjoy Janet Tronstad's *Stranded with Santa* (#1626), a fun-loving romp about a rodeo megastar who gets stormbound with a beautiful young widow. Then, discover how to melt a Scrooge's heart in Moyra Tarling's *Christmas Due Date* (#1629)

I hope you enjoy these stories, and please keep in touch!

Mary-Theresa Hussey

Mary-Theresa Hussey
Senior Editor

Please address questions and book requests to:
Silhouette Reader Service
U.S.: 3010 Walden Ave., P.O. Box 1325, Buffalo, NY 14269
Canadian: P.O. Box 609, Fort Erie, Ont. L2A 5X3

The Baron & the Bodyguard

VALERIE PARV

Published by Silhouette Books

America's Publisher of Contemporary Romance

For my wonderful sister-in-law, Helga.

ISBN 0-373-19627-X

THE BARON & THE BODYGUARD

This edition published by arrangement with Harlequin Books S.A.

Visit Silhouette at www.eHarlequin.com

Printed in U.S.A.

Books by Valerie Parv

Silhouette Romance

The Leopard Tree #507
The Billionaire's Baby Chase #1270
Baby Wishes and Bachelor Kisses #1313
**The Monarch's Son* #1459
**The Prince's Bride-To-Be* #1465
**The Princess's Proposal* #1471
Booties and the Beast #1501
Code Name: Prince #1516
†*Crowns and a Cradle* #1621
†*The Baron & the Bodyguard* #1627

Silhouette Intimate Moments

Interrupted Lullaby #1095
Royal Spy #1154

*The Carramer Crown
†The Carramer Legacy

VALERIE PARV

lives and breathes romance and has even written a guide to being romantic, crediting her cartoonist husband of nearly thirty years as her inspiration. As a former buffalo and crocodile hunter in Australia's Northern Territory, he's ready-made hero material, she says.

When not writing her novels and nonfiction books, or speaking about romance on Australian radio and television, Valerie enjoys dollhouses, being a *Star Trek* fan and playing with food (in cooking, that is). Valerie agrees with actor Nichelle Nichols who said, "The difference between fantasy and fact is that fantasy simply hasn't happened yet."

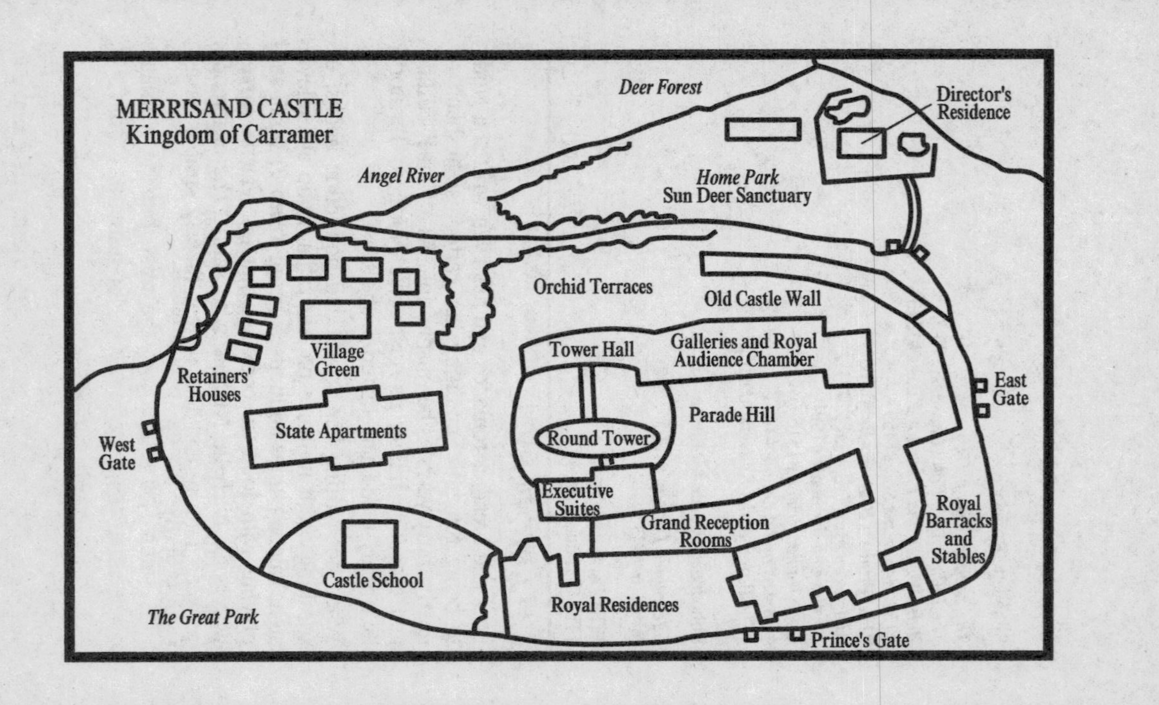
MERRISAND CASTLE
Kingdom of Carramer
Deer Forest
Director's Residence
Angel River
Home Park
Sun Deer Sanctuary
Orchid Terraces
Old Castle Wall
Village Green
Tower Hall
Galleries and Royal Audience Chamber
Retainers' Houses
East Gate
Parade Hill
State Apartments
West Gate
Round Tower
Executive Suites
Grand Reception Rooms
Royal Barracks and Stables
Castle School
Royal Residences
The Great Park
Prince's Gate

Chapter One

Mathiaz was floating.

Pain shredded the edges of the mist surrounding him, but he found if he concentrated, he could push the pain away and enjoy the sensation of nothingness. Of floating free of care.

"Come on, Baron, don't do this to me."

The woman's voice punched through the mist, bringing the awareness of pain closer. Pushing the pain away meant pushing her away, too, and for some reason, he didn't want her to go, so he let both of them in. Immediately fire tore along the side of his leg, and every muscle in his body set up a clamoring ache as though from overuse. He heard a distant groan that he barely recognized as coming from himself.

He wanted to retreat into the mist, but the woman's voice came again, refusing to let him go. "That's it, come back to me. You can do it."

Come back where? To whom? He couldn't force the questions out, but she anticipated them. "It's me, Jac.

You're in the hospital. You have to wake up for my sake, Mathiaz."

Jac? Instinctively he rejected the name. Jacinta, that felt better. He remembered that her name was Jacinta Newnham, although she liked to be called Jac. He must have murmured her name, because her sigh whispered over him.

He felt her bend closer, and her lips brushed his mouth. A faint scent of frangipani teased his nostrils, the perfume as familiar as her touch and every bit as arousing. The sensation was so pleasant that he took it with him back into the mist.

Jacinta felt his grip slacken and fought back tears as she looked at Mathiaz in the bed. The nightmare was happening all over again. A man she cared about was hovering on the brink, and there was nothing she could do. For a moment, she'd thought she'd managed to reach him, only to watch him sink back into coma.

A white-coated man came to stand beside Mathiaz's bed. "Isn't it time you got some rest?"

She gave the doctor a savage look. "I'm not going anywhere until he comes out of this, Dr. Pascale."

"I know I asked you to come in and talk to him, but running yourself into the ground isn't going to help anyone."

"Then tell me what will?"

The doctor's craggy face softened. "With all the medical marvels at our disposal, sometimes there's nothing you can do but wait."

Nothing you can do. The words she hated most in the whole world. "There must be something."

"You're doing it. Keep talking to him, let him know

you're here and that there's a world he should be rejoining by now."

"Talk to him about what?"

The doctor thought for a moment. "You worked with him for four months. Talk about the time you spent together."

"That ended ten months ago. We didn't part on very good terms."

"He fired you?"

She shook her head. "He wanted me to stay. I was the one who quit."

"Didn't take to royal life, huh?"

"The baron hired me for a specific assignment. When the danger to him was past, I had no reason to stay." She didn't tell the doctor that Mathiaz had given her the one reason guaranteed to make her run like a rabbit. He had begun to care about her.

The doctor's expression showed he had his own suspicions. "I got the impression that the two of you..."

She didn't let him finish. "We set out to create that impression as a cover. Mathiaz thought that being seen with increased security would alarm the public. Running my own defense academy, I have the skills but I'm not actually a bodyguard, so he suggested I pose as his girlfriend while keeping him from harm."

The doctor looked at her as if he didn't quite believe her, but decided to let it go. "Then talk to him about yourself."

"He already knows my background. He had palace security check me out before I came aboard."

"I don't mean the facts, I mean you, your interests, your passions. You do have passions, don't you?"

She kept her face averted. What would the doctor say if she admitted that one of her passions had been Mathiaz himself? "Climbing and adventure training," she said instead.

The doctor made a skeptical noise. "I've heard you took two American teenagers to ride the Nuee Trail, but I've never heard having a death wish described as a passion before."

"Depends how much you care about what you're doing. Those boys were tough street kids. A judge gave them the choice of undertaking one of my adventure training courses to straighten themselves out, or going to jail."

"I'd take jail."

She knew the doctor didn't mean it. As court physician, Alain Pascale was known for his gruff manner, but also for his willingness to do anything he could to help his patients. "Anyway, I didn't take them out solo. The court supplied a supervisor who complained all the way up and down the mountain. The boys acted tough but they were only sixteen and seventeen," she told him.

"The age when Carramer males traditionally ride the Nuee Trail," the doctor mused. "They considered it a rite of passage for hundreds of years."

"As well as being one of the toughest endurance rides in the world," she pointed out. "When those boys finished the course, they were different people." She had also been different, too, in love with an island kingdom called Carramer. She had returned to America long enough to resign from her job as a personal trainer, said a tearful goodbye to her parents and older sister and moved to Carramer. When suitable premises in Valmont came up for rent, she had leased it and spent the next three years establishing her own fitness business. Guarding Mathiaz had seemed like an interesting change of pace at the time.

The doctor patted her shoulder. "Now you know what to talk to the baron about."

"This feels weird," she said to the still form in the bed after the doctor had gone. "While I worked for you, we talked so much, but I managed to tell you very little about myself."

He had asked, she remembered, but she hadn't wanted to let him get too close. She still wasn't prepared to tell him the most significant details of her life. He might be unconscious but she preferred to keep some secrets.

"There isn't much to tell," she began awkwardly. "Compared to your royal family, mine isn't the least bit glamorous. Mom and Dad have a berry farm in Orange County, California, and my sister, Debbie, runs a store selling their produce and local handicrafts when she isn't taking care of her husband and their three children. She's much better suited to that life than me, although I never thought I'd end up on an island in the middle of the South Pacific."

She lapsed into silence. Once she had thought of training as a kindergarten teacher. She enjoyed working with children, the reason she'd volunteered to help the street kids in her spare time. Switching her degree from education to science, with a major in sport and exercise had been an impulsive choice. The right one, as things turned out. At twenty-seven, she was still a teacher of sorts, and exercise was a universal skill, as useful in Carramer as in Orange County.

"I'm supposed to talk to you about passion. How's that for irony?" she asked Mathiaz's unmoving form. She felt a pang as she said the word. Mathiaz had been a passionate man—*was* a passionate man, she amended the thought firmly. They had agreed to act in public as if there was a romance between them. Holding hands, exchanging looks, all in the name of keeping him safe.

When had they stopped acting?

The first time he kissed her, she remembered. Two months after she started working for him, she had accompanied him to a trade dinner. Hardly a forum for passion. In the back of the limousine, returning to Château Valmont, they had laughed about how boring the chief delegate's speech had been. Letting Mathiaz kiss her had seemed like the most natural thing in the world.

He'd kissed her again as they shared a nightcap at his villa in the royal compound. Talked long into the night. Talked some more the next day. Kissed again. She had told herself she was acting a part, while recognizing the lie for what it was.

She should have left after the man threatening Mathiaz was caught, but she'd agreed to stay for another month, telling herself she needed the pay check. The truth was, she needed Mathiaz. And she didn't want to need any man.

Unconscious, he was no threat to her peace of mind, she told herself. When she had agreed to Dr. Pascale's request to help Mathiaz, she hadn't counted on the strength of her own feelings at being so close to him. She dragged a hand through her hair. When she'd walked into the room, found him tangled in tubes and medical monitors, her heart had almost stopped.

She'd taken his hand without thinking, unprepared for the electric jolt that arced through her. His fingers had closed around hers so strongly that she had to remind herself he was unconscious. He'd felt as if he was holding on to her. According to Dr. Pascale, he possibly was.

She cleared her throat. "Dr. Pascale asked me what's my passion? Being strong, having answers. Only this time I don't have any. He thinks I can help you by talking to you. But you have to do your part. You have to wake up.''

The man on the bed stirred, his fingers flexing. With a sigh she slid her hand into his, and he seemed to settle. She wished she could say the same for herself, but the pulse at her throat fluttered like a trapped bird, and she could feel her heart hammering. She told herself she was scared for Mathiaz, but knew some of her discomfort was for herself. For the pleasure she felt at his touch and didn't want to feel. Could you turn off feelings by wanting to? In the ten months since she'd left him, she'd tried with everything in her. Thought she had succeeded. Knew she was kidding herself the moment she walked into his hospital room.

She still cared about him, and it scared the life out of her.

She untangled her fingers from his and straightened. ''I'm sorry, Mathiaz, but I can't do this anymore. I have to go.'' His eyelids began to quiver.

Mathiaz had no idea how long he drifted, dreaming of the woman called Jacinta. Gradually he became aware that she was calling to him more and more urgently. He grasped her hand because the gesture seemed natural. How warm and soft she felt, but she wasn't, he knew. How did he know that?

This time he was able to force his eyes open, and saw a vision bending over him. Jacinta. A head sculpted by Michelangelo was capped with shining blond hair, neat except for a few stray wisps curling across her forehead and around her ears. The effect suggested an abandoned nature kept under firm control, but not quite. His blurred gaze gave him an imperfect view of her unusual gray-blue eyes, enough to see that they glistened, as if she was trying not to cry.

He moved restively, wanting to stroke her lovely face, to reassure her that tears were unnecessary. He was fine. But his arms were held to his sides by a web of tubes. He couldn't summon the energy to wonder what flowed through the tubes, or why they snaked into his veins. He was too busy trying to focus on what Jacinta was saying to him.

His hold on consciousness was too precarious to sort out her words, so he concentrated on her generous mouth, finding that he remembered exactly how her lips felt against his own, and how much heat her touch could ignite inside him. He groaned again, this time with the remembered pleasure of holding her, caressing her. In the vestiges of his floating cocoon, the image was so vivid that he raised himself to take her into his arms, desperate to turn the dream of closeness into reality.

She pressed against his shoulders, settling him back. "Don't try to move, you've been hurt."

As if he hadn't worked that out for himself. He didn't normally wake up in this much of a mess. "What..." he tried hoarsely. His mouth was too arid for speech.

She lifted his head and slid ice chips into his mouth. The coolness eased the burning in his throat, but not in his body. The brush of her fingers against his lips made him ache to embrace her and kiss her again.

Again? Had he really kissed her, or only in his dream? Surely if he was dreaming, he should be able to control the outcome? Which didn't include being pinned to a bed, restricted to looking at his ministering angel, when his imagination stretched to far more enjoyable ways they could spend the time.

"I see our patient is finally coming around. Nice work, Ms. Newnham."

The gravel voice dissipated some of the mist surrounding Mathiaz, and he felt the pain settle around him like a cloak, unable to be pushed away. His vision cleared, revealing a steel-haired man in a white coat looming above him, coming between Mathiaz and the angelic vision. Mathiaz made an involuntary sound of protest as the doctor checked him over with professional skill.

When he finished, he peered intently at Mathiaz. "Do you know who you are?"

Mathiaz croaked out an unsuccessful reply, coughed, and tried again with better results. "Mathiaz Albert Alphonse de Marigny, Baron Montravel."

The doctor's concerned expression eased, although it was hard to tell because his face was as craggy as clothing that had been slept in for several days. "Beats me how you remember all that even when you're not injured. Now who am I?"

This was much easier to answer. "A pain in the neck."

The doctor shot a relieved look at Jacinta. "He's himself all right. Like the rest of the de Marigny family, he has no respect for my medical skills. You'd think I'd be entitled to some respect after bringing most of them into the world, Lord Montravel here included."

Alain Pascale, personal physician to Mathiaz's cousin, Prince Lorne, ruler of Carramer, Mathiaz's mind slowly supplied the details. The doctor had served the family for decades, as he said delivering many of the royal babies in that time. He was the only man in Carramer who could speak so familiarly to members of the royal family, his unique place in their affections giving him immunity from the demands of protocol. He wasn't above taking advantage of it when he thought one of the family needed his guidance, Mathiaz knew. But the doctor was semiretired now. Whatever Mathiaz had gotten himself into must have been drastic to drag the doctor away from his beloved orchid growing.

''What happened?'' he struggled to ask.

The doctor shook his head. ''Plenty of time for that. Right now, you need rest.''

Pascale did something to the equipment beside Mathiaz's bed and he felt himself slipping back into sleep. He didn't resist. Jacinta waited for him there.

Chapter Two

When next Mathiaz awoke, some of the pain has dissipated and he felt stronger. Sunlight streamed across the room. He recalled it had been dark when last he awoke. He must have slept around the clock.

He turned his head, smiling at the sight of his ministering angel seated beside his bed. She was asleep and looked even more beautiful than she had in his dreams.

Within minutes of the medical equipment registering his return to consciousness, Dr. Pascale hurried to his side. Instantly Jacinta stirred and came to her feet almost in the same moment. "Is something wrong?" she asked the doctor.

"You can ask our patient," Pascale said with a smile.

"Mathiaz, you're awake."

Wishing he knew what he'd done to deserve the look of delight on her face, Mathiaz managed to nod. "Looks like it."

"Do you know what happened?" Dr. Pascale asked.

Mathiaz struggled to think around the fog in his mind. The answer refused to come.

The doctor rested his fingers against Mathiaz's wrist and frowned at the fast-beating pulse Mathiaz could feel from the inside. "Don't agitate yourself. It will come back," the doctor assured him.

"You were on your way to the royal treasury. You were caught in an explosion," Jacinta supplied.

"Accident?" Mathiaz asked. Surely he should be able to remember such an event? When he tried, he met only blankness.

"The police and palace security are still investigating," she said, but her expression told him she had her own theory. "If I'd been working for you..."

He narrowed his eyes. "Why weren't you? You're my bodyguard."

She and the doctor exchanged concerned looks before the doctor asked, "What's the last thing you remember before waking up here?"

Mathiaz had to think. "Taking Prince Henry some books for his nurse to read to him."

"Prince Henry?" she said, sounding troubled.

Mathiaz's uncle, Prince Henry, ruled Valmont Province under an ancient charter granted to the de Valmont family by the Carramer crown. "You should remember. You came with me."

She took his hand, her grip warm and firm in his. "Mathiaz, the day you remember happened over a year ago. Henry died six months ago. In his will, he left you the Antoinette wedding ring. You were on your way to the treasury to have the ring valued when you were caught in the explosion."

Mathiaz clung to her hand, wondering why holding her felt so right. Henry hadn't been anyone's favorite member of the family, but he and Mathiaz had respected each other. The old prince didn't deserve to have his death erased from Mathiaz's memory.

"What are you talking about? As far as I know, we saw my uncle yesterday. If he's gone, then who..."

Her touch soothed some of his agitation. "Your cousin, Prince Josquin de Marigny, rules the province as Crown Regent until his stepson, Christophe, comes of age," she anticipated his question.

That meant Josquin had married Sarah de Valmont, the American-born princess who had grown up in an adoptive family and borne Prince Henry an heir without knowing that she was Henry's granddaughter, Mathiaz worked out. Their wedding and Josquin's elevation to the Regency had vanished from his memory as if they had never taken place. He had missed baby Christophe's accession to the throne, his cousin's wedding, everything.

"How long have I been here?" he asked.

The doctor looked up from the chart he was studying. "You were brought in the day before yesterday. We worked on your injuries for a couple of hours, then you were semicomatose for another twelve and sleeping the rest. All up, you've been here two and a half days."

"So how can I have lost a year?"

The doctor came closer, chart in hand. "My diagnosis is post-traumatic amnesia. Happens a lot in cases of closed-head injuries and shock. The mind can't deal with what happened so it skips backward, to a more tolerable memory, giving the brain time to develop coping mechanisms."

"You mean that whole year of my life is just... gone?" Mathiaz let his tone reflect his disbelief.

"Sounds that way. There's no sign of any physical

injury to the brain, but you were knocked unconscious by the blast, striking your head against the carved doors of the treasury as you fell. I'll consult a specialist, since this is out of my field, but she'll probably confirm my diagnosis."

No wonder Mathiaz felt as if a team of miners were drilling through his brain. The treasury doors were eight feet tall and almost as wide, and made of foot-thick iron-wood. "No physical injury? That means my memory is intact. All I have to do is recover it, right?"

Dr. Pascale nodded. "That's the good news."

Mathiaz's gut clenched involuntarily. "And the bad?"

"I can't say when you might get your memory back."

Mathiaz refused to accept that his memory of everything that had taken place in the last year was gone forever. Giving up wasn't in his vocabulary. But some things were beyond even willpower. "You mean I might never recover those memories?"

"You have to consider the possibility."

Mathiaz's anger warred with his confusion. Having a headache the size of Carramer didn't help. "What about hypnosis, therapy of some kind?" he demanded.

The doctor sighed. "This kind of retrograde amnesia is the mind's way of dealing with the stress of major trauma. Trying to force a recovery could do more harm than good. Better to let yourself remember in your own sweet time."

"Or not." Mathiaz's voice was edged with bitterness.

"Or not." The doctor's professionally calm expression didn't change. Only his pale blue eyes registered the depths of his concern. "Give yourself time to recover before you start worrying too much."

"Easy for you to say, Dr. Pascale. You don't have a hole where the last year of your life is supposed to be."

"It could be worse. The hole could have been in your head, if not for..."

"The angle of the explosion," Jacinta said, cutting the doctor off in midsentence. "Another few feet closer to the source and you wouldn't be here to complain about a few lost memories."

Mathiaz intercepted a look between the two that he couldn't interpret. Annoyed at being so obviously excluded, he glanced at the tubes feeding into his arm. "Are these really necessary?"

The doctor snapped the chart shut and replaced it at the foot of the bed. "One thing you didn't acquire in the last year is a medical degree, Lord Montravel." He made the title sound vaguely insulting. "I'll be the judge of what you need and when you need it. Now just lie there and be glad you're still in one piece."

Jacinta asked, "Is he always this abrasive?"

Mathiaz grinned tiredly. "The time to worry is when he starts being nice."

The doctor growled a negation. "You were easier to deal with when you were asleep." But he managed to sound pleased at the same time.

"What else has happened that I don't remember?"

"I'll let Ms. Newnham fill you in on whatever you want to know. She's the specialist when it comes to Lord Montravel. I have work to do."

The doctor left and Mathiaz turned his head toward Jacinta. "What did he mean, you're the specialist on me?"

She looked uncomfortable. "When they had trouble getting you to wake up after the surgery, Dr. Pascale called me in, hoping that I could get through to you."

She had succeeded better than she knew, but her impersonal manner made him wonder if his erotic fantasies about her were just that, fantasies. "Why did he have to call you in? Don't you work for me anymore?"

She glanced at the surgical monitors over Mathiaz's bed. The readings evidently gave her cause for concern, because she said, "We don't have to cover everything now. You should get some rest."

His hand clamped around her wrist. "From the sound of things, I've had too much rest. I want to know what went on between us."

Something flared in her unusual eyes, but was gone before he could identify it. "Nothing went on between us, as you put it. Fourteen months ago, you hired me following a security scare at the Château Valmont. Your valet, Andre Zenio, was fired for showing people around the palace without clearing them with the Royal Protection Detail. Zenio blamed you for getting him fired, although you weren't the one who reported him. He started stalking you and making threats. Eventually the police caught him, and I went back to my work at the academy. End of story."

Mathiaz remembered most of this. He knew that she ran a personal defense school in Valmont's capital city of Perla. Mathiaz's younger brother, Eduard, had taught a course at the academy and came back singing Jacinta's praises. When Mathiaz started getting threats and being followed, the police advised hiring extra security. Jacinta had been the logical choice. She had the appropriate skills, but could be presented as Mathiaz's girlfriend rather than as a bodyguard, saving the need to go public about the security scare.

"There was nothing more between us?" he asked, wondering why the question sounded so ridiculous, as if part of him already knew that there was.

She hesitated. "We were attracted to one another."

Why did he get the feeling that was the understatement of the year? He sure as blazes was attracted to her, but in the incendiary kind of way that usually ended up in bed. He could hardly believe that she didn't share his feelings. "How far did we take this—attraction?" he asked.

"We didn't."

Was he imagining things, or was her answer a little too glib? "I don't believe you."

She sketched a bow from the neck. "You have the right to believe what you choose, Lord Montravel."

Pain fueled his irritation. "You can drop the Lord Montravel bit. We both know you never call me anything but Mathiaz or Baron when we're alone." They were alone now.

"As you wish, Baron."

Her ready agreement didn't fool him, either. "I may have forgotten the last year of my life, but I remember you were never awed by my rank and titles."

"I'm an American, I was brought up in a democracy," she reminded him, as if her California accent hadn't already done so. "We don't believe in bowing and scraping."

He doubted if she would bow or scrape to anyone, regardless of her nationality. "You sure you're not related to Alain Pascale?" he asked.

"Only by attitude." She hefted a capacious shoulder bag off a chair. "I'd better leave you to get some rest."

He felt the need to keep her with him. "What brought you to Carramer?"

She hesitated. "We have talked about this before."

"Humor me."

"Carramer is a beautiful, peaceful kingdom, and Valmont province is one of the most attractive regions."

"With about as much use for a self-defense expert as a fish has for a bicycle," he pointed out. Apart from an occasional problem like the security scare, Carramer had one of the lowest crime rates in the world. What wasn't she telling him?

She shrugged. "Maybe that's why I wanted to live here. The skills I teach are as useful for honing self-discipline and fitness as they are for fighting crime."

If all her pupils developed figures like hers, he could hardly argue. She had moved a little away and she stood about five-eight, although trapped on the bed, he couldn't see if that was with or without heels. With, his memory supplied. Without, he recalled, she only came up to his shoulder.

She had a waist he could nearly span with two hands, although he'd need a longer reach to span any higher. She was dressed in a clinging sunshine-yellow halter top that left her satiny shoulders bare and emphasized the fullness of her feminine curves. The top was tucked into the slimmest pair of black denim jeans he'd seen in a long time. Getting into them must be an exercise in itself, he thought, then slammed a lid on the thought. Trussed up as he was, letting himself dwell on such things was a recipe for terminal frustration.

"Why did you agree to come back?" he asked, hoping she'd give him a clue as to why she'd left his employ in the first place.

She looked startled as if the question was unexpected. "You needed me," she said. Then she glanced away as if she had given away more than she wanted to.

He felt a surge of satisfaction. "If you were from Carramer, I could put your answer down to loyalty to the crown, but you're not. You tell me there's nothing between us, yet you come running the moment I'm injured. Does that sound like nothing to you?"

"You always did twist my words," she snapped. "I've a good mind to…"

"Careful," he cautioned her. "You're dealing with an injured man."

"He'll be a lot worse injured if he keeps provoking me."

"Does the word 'treason' mean anything to you?" he asked, pleased to have provoked some sort of response from her.

She wrapped her arms around herself as if she was cold. "As I recall, you threatened to have me charged with treason when I resigned. It didn't work then, so I don't see why it should change my behavior now."

"I didn't want you to leave?"

The question hung in the air between them. Finally she shook her head. "No, but you didn't need a bodyguard after Zenio was caught."

He must have had another reason for wanting her to stay, he concluded. He wished his head didn't ache so abominably, making thinking such an ordeal. Belatedly he noticed something else. She wore a flesh-colored bandage on her left forearm. She saw him looking at it and dropped the arm to her side, where she'd held it since he woke up, wanting to keep him from seeing the injury, he assumed.

"How did you come by that?"

She glanced at the bandage then looked away. "It's nothing. I was jogging past the treasury at the time of the bombing."

He hated the thought of her being injured, however slightly. "You weren't working for me, so what were you doing there?"

She had been running through the park and had seen him approach the treasury in his limousine. Even as she chided herself for acting like a sycophantic teenager, she had moved closer, hoping for another glimpse of him when he got out.

Automatically her gaze had swept the area. Her realization that something was wrong had been almost subliminal, an awareness that one of the terra-cotta pots of flowers edging the steps didn't match the others. It was also out of alignment, as if it had been added in haste.

She had moved without conscious thought, grabbing the object and flinging it into the lake. Before the water could absorb the detonation the bomb hidden in the pot had exploded in the air, the blast catching Mathiaz as he walked up the treasury steps.

A flying fragment of hot debris had singed her arm, but she hadn't paid the injury any attention until later. At the time, she had been consumed with worry for Mathiaz. Seeing him stir and moan, she had known he was still alive, and it had been all she could do not to rush to his side.

No one had seen her action, or if they had, they hadn't reported her to the police because she hadn't been detained or interviewed. She had waited long enough to see a doctor emerge from the crowd and check Mathiaz over then an ambulance had arrived and she had slipped away. Later she had telephoned the police and tipped them off about the flowerpot, without identifying herself.

Explaining about her role to the police or to Mathiaz would have meant revealing her feelings for him. She was far from ready for that, so she said, "When I saw your car pull up, I was curious to see what you were doing, that's all."

Her answer left him unsatisfied, as if he suspected

there was more she wasn't telling him. "You weren't keeping an informal eye on me, by any chance?"

Her heightened color told him he was getting close, but she shook her head. "I told you, I was only called in after you became injured. Dr. Pascale hoped a familiar face would help bring you back to consciousness."

"The family is full of familiar faces. Any one of them could have answered Pascale's call as well as you could. There's another reason, isn't there?"

This time she met his gaze. "The police are treating the explosion as suspicious, so palace security asked me to come back for the time being."

An upsurge of pleasure at the news that she was staying around, was offset by the worry her statement generated. Apart from an occasional malcontent like Zenio, Carramer had few antiroyalists. Fewer still who would actively harm the monarchy which ensured the country's peace and prosperity. Mathiaz asked grimly, "What do you think?"

Her expression tightened. "Explosions don't happen by themselves. We'll know more when the experts have finished combing through the debris. The treasury portico and front courtyard were a mess."

He fisted handfuls of the bedclothes, his tension rising. "Was anyone else hurt?"

"A couple of passersby had near misses. Mostly shock. As luck would have it, you arrived a few minutes early. The staff were on their way to greet you when the explosion occurred."

"Then I should thank my stars we all got off so lightly." Another thought occurred to him. "I did get off lightly, didn't I? There's nothing Pascale hasn't told me?"

"Your leg is still attached, if that's what's worrying

you,'' she assured him. She gave a knowing smile. ''And according to Dr. Pascale, everything else is in working order.''

Mathiaz masked his relief. As far as he could remember, he wasn't involved with anyone, but he hoped one day to have a wife and children, especially a son to inherit his land and titles. Jacinta's oblique reassurance meant they were still a possibility.

Good grief, he could be married already, and not remember. The thought made him realize how much could have happened in the months he had lost. He felt awkward asking Jacinta whether or not he was involved with anyone, so he kept silent. Surely if he had, she would have been at his bedside, rather than Jacinta?

''What happened to my leg?'' he asked instead.

''They removed a chunk of shrapnel from your calf muscle, so you won't be playing hopscotch for a week or so. You'll be on crutches for another week, but after that, with care, you should heal as good as new.''

Some of his anxiety receded. ''What about your arm?''

''It's nothing.''

''One thing I do remember is that with you, nothing can cover anything from a bruise to the need for a bionic replacement.''

A smile blossomed, lighting up her features, and Mathiaz felt his insides tighten. In the months she'd worked with him—a year ago now, he struggled to remember—she hadn't smiled nearly often enough. When she did, it was like the sun coming out. He felt an aching need to see her smile again.

''Were we lovers?''

Instead of making her smile, his question had her looking away. He felt cheated. In his dream when he'd held her in his arms, his mouth hungry on hers, she'd laughed with happiness. She'd responded out of her own hunger, and the ferocity of what they'd shared made him ache with the desire to translate dream into reality.

"If you weren't injured, I'd be insulted," she said. "It wouldn't say much for my lovemaking capability if you couldn't remember."

She hadn't answered his question, he noticed, wondering if her brittle response covered something deeper. More wishful thinking? Or a memory beyond conscious reach? He decided to match her brittleness, for now. "Considering I can't remember what I had for breakfast, it's hardly an insult."

"French toast and double-strength black coffee."

He stared at her. As far as he knew, that was the breakfast he'd eaten, except that it wasn't yesterday, it was months ago. "How did you..."

"You have the same thing every morning except Sundays when you have eggs Benedict."

Inwardly he felt gratified at how well she knew him. Warning himself not to read too much into the discovery, he said, "Am I that predictable?"

"Bad security, but yes. When I worked for you, we argued a lot about the need to vary your routines to reduce the risk of the stalker being able to predict your movements."

The relationship he remembered was friendly but formal, at least on Jacinta's side. On his own, he remembered a strong wish to turn their association into something more personal. Had they done so, or had it remained another dream? "I don't recall arguing with you."

"Trust me, we didn't see eye to eye on anything much."

She had revealed more than she knew, Mathiaz thought. He rarely argued with anyone. When they were boys, his brother, Eduard, used to complain that Mathiaz preferred to use logic rather than fists to resolve their differences. No wonder Eduard had ended up a navy pilot, while Mathiaz had gone into government.

Mathiaz wondered if Jacinta knew how much she had just revealed. For sparks to have flown between them, she had to have reached him on a level few people did. Their relationship may have started out purely professional, but somewhere along the line things had changed, he would swear to it. He was still agonizing over it when a nurse came in, smiled at him, and did something to the drip feeding into his arm, before making a note on his chart. Moments later, he was deeply asleep.

Jacinta wondered if he sensed her keeping watch at his side.

Chapter Three

"This...is...not...my...idea...of...fun," Jacinta said around a plastic mouthguard, punctuating each word with vicious right and left jabs at a leather covered punching bag suspended from the ceiling of Mathiaz's private gymnasium.

Being surrounded by an army of servants gave her a lot of sympathy for people who needed bodyguards all the time. Until she came to work for the baron the first time, she had never understood how annoying it was to have someone shadowing her every move. She had only been back at Château Valmont for two weeks, and already she longed for the freedom to come and go without having people underfoot constantly.

The gymnasium was one of the few places she could have privacy. Attendants were on call at the press of a button, along with a personal trainer, a masseur, and for all she knew, someone to do the workout for her. But at least they weren't in the same room watching every move she made.

Security cameras scrutinized the perimeter of the complex, but Mathiaz had vetoed their presence inside the workout rooms themselves. On security grounds, Jacinta should object, but right now she was glad no one could see her work off her frustration.

She didn't like living in the royal compound, and she didn't like being on call for Mathiaz twenty-four hours a day, knowing she was the only one who remembered everything they'd shared. She launched a roundhouse punch at the bag. The recoil almost knocked her off her feet, but the release of tension felt good.

The baron had been discharged from the hospital after a week, using crutches for the first week. Now his leg had all but healed and he could get around using only a stick until he regained full strength.

He had thrown himself into his recovery with his usual determination. Challenged by Dr. Pascale to get back on his feet in two weeks, he managed it in less. Confronted with a physiotherapy program that would make a lesser man blanch, he had followed it to the letter, although Jacinta hadn't missed the clenched teeth and sweat-soaked clothing that accompanied his progress.

She only wished as much progress had been made identifying the reason for the explosion. The combined efforts of the police and the royal protection detail hadn't turned up anything useful. No demands had been received at the château. A group of hotheads claiming responsibility would have given them some leads, but there was nothing.

The police had interviewed the employee who had threatened Mathiaz before. Zenio was on parole, but the police found no connection, although Jacinta thought there had to be one. In a country as peaceful as Carramer, two lots of threats against the same member of the royal family was stretching coincidence. But she had no evidence, only suspicions.

She took another swing at the punching bag. How did you fight an invisible enemy?

"You must have killed that bag by now."

She shoved the mouthguard into a pocket and pushed locks of sweat-streaked hair off her forehead, then tried for an impersonal tone. "Good morning, Baron. Has Dr. Pascale finished with you already?"

Mathiaz rubbed his chin ruefully. "He accused me of wasting his time, his way of telling me I'm doing fine."

He gestured toward the punching bag. "You're attacking that as if it's a mortal enemy."

She reached for a towel and hung it around her neck. "You never know, someday it might be."

"Have you ever tried talking your way out of a jam?"

She swabbed her face with the towel. "Sometimes talking doesn't work." And sometimes it got people killed, she thought but didn't say.

Mathiaz rested his stick against a wall, let his silk robe pool on the floor, and dropped onto a bench, positioning himself to perform the exercises the physiotherapist had prescribed. She saw him wince as he stretched and flexed his injured leg, but he kept up the movements until sweat beaded his face.

He might not believe in fighting his way out of a crisis, but he fought when he had to. She had never seen anyone attack a rehabilitation program so single-mindedly. At thirty-one, he had a superb physique thanks to his passions for climbing and bushwalking, and his fitness stood him in good stead now.

Watching him work out, she almost wished he looked less imposing. It was all too easy to remember how his strong arms had held her, and to want him to hold her again.

She stopped the punching bag's pendulum action, stripped off her gloves, and crossed the room to a state-of-the-art walking machine.

"How's the arm?" he asked, grunting as he hefted a set of weights resting against his ankles.

She fiddled with the settings on the treadmill. "Fine." The bandage had been replaced by a smaller sticking plaster, the burn itself already fading.

He lowered the weights and sat up, straddling the bench. "I still have trouble believing that you were in the vicinity of the explosion by pure coincidence."

"Coincidence or not, it's true." Her guarded tone sounded betraying even to her.

He heard it, too. "I could pull royal rank and make you tell me more."

"You can't, I'm not a Carramer citizen. All you can do is have me thrown out of the country."

"Don't tempt me," he growled. "You live here, you have a business here, yet you haven't taken out citizenship. Don't you plan on staying?"

A few months ago her answer would have been an unequivocal yes. Now, she wasn't sure. Before the explosion, she had been thinking of selling the academy. The woman who helped manage it had expressed an interest. Jacinta could return to her native California and...do what? Martial arts experts were a dime a dozen in the States. So were self-defense classes and personal trainers. She wasn't guaranteed a good living, and definitely not the exotic surroundings she enjoyed in Perla, the largest city in Valmont Province, where her home and business were located.

Who was she kidding? She didn't stay in Carramer

because of her work or the tropical scenery, but because Mathiaz was here. She had done the one thing she knew bodyguards weren't supposed to do, get involved with their clients. Judgment got clouded, mistakes were made. People got hurt.

Like Mathiaz.

Never mind that she wasn't a professional. She was acting as one. If she hadn't allowed her own fears to drive her away, she would still have been working for him when the explosion happened, and been able to prevent him from being injured. As if it could expiate her guilt, Jacinta wrenched the dial on the treadmill all the way around, giving herself an uphill hike that left her panting within minutes.

The pressure slackened abruptly as Mathiaz twisted the dial lower. She grabbed the side rails and slowed her pace to match the treadmill's dwindling speed. "Why did you do that?"

"You can't talk when you're climbing Everest."

"Who says I want to talk?"

"You may not, but I do. Since I got out of the hospital I've been treated with kid gloves by everyone but you."

She gave him what her Scottish grandmother would have called an old-fashioned look. "Are you complaining?"

"The opposite. You have my full permission to go on giving me a hard time."

A smile tugged at the corners of her mouth. "I don't recall ever needing your permission. But this is the first time you've considered it beneficial. May I ask the reason?"

"I want to get back to normal as fast as possible. Mollycoddling isn't going to achieve it."

"Whereas being taunted and nagged provides a better

incentive,'' she guessed. She remembered that he worked best under pressure, setting his own goals and deadlines, and taking satisfaction in exceeding those set by others. She stepped off the treadmill and gestured to a padded floor area in one corner. ''It's a shame you can't join me in a few falls—in the interests of not mollycoddling you.''

While guarding him the last time, she had jogged with him, worked out in the gym with him, but never invited him to join her in practicing any of the defense disciplines in which she was trained. The warrior arts created a physical closeness between the combatants that was more than she dared to encourage between herself and Mathiaz, not that resisting had done her much good.

She wasn't sure why she wished he could join her now. Telling herself she was complying with his order to push him to his limits might explain his motives, but it didn't explain hers.

Mathiaz looked at the mat speculatively. ''Might be interesting at that.''

She had only made the comment because she thought it was impossible. ''I'm sure Dr. Pascale's prescription doesn't include martial arts,'' she said, hoping he would agree and give her a graceful way out of this.

Mathiaz's jaw hardened as he compared her small size against his own well-muscled bulk. His stay in the hospital hadn't done much to even the odds between them. ''Pascale gave me the all-clear to do anything I feel up to doing. You should be more worried that I might hurt you.''

He had already done so in ways he couldn't imagine. Throwing her over his shoulder a few times couldn't do much more damage. ''In your dreams, Baron,'' she said.

"Haven't you heard the saying that size isn't everything?"

She regretted starting down that path when she saw his eyes glitter. "All depends on the arena," he said softly and closed the distance between them.

She drew a ragged breath, feeling cornered. "Shouldn't we get changed?"

"There's something I want to do first."

The air seemed charged, and she had difficulty catching her breath. She knew it had nothing to do with her workout on the treadmill, and everything to do with the man standing so close to her she could see the tiny flecks of gold in his blue eyes.

He had lost a little weight since the explosion, and the aristocratic angles of his face were more sharply defined than ever, adding to his devastating appeal. Though his ordeal had etched lines of strain around his mouth, renewed energy radiated from him. He stood easily, his injured leg taking his weight almost evenly with his good leg. She let her eyes close, knowing that he meant to kiss her, and knowing equally well that she was going to let him.

Ten months of self-imposed exile from him had taken a toll. She told herself she wanted to feel his touch for old times' sake, to give her something to remember him by when this was over, and they went their separate ways again.

The moment his arms came around her and he pulled her against his chest, she knew she lied.

Her cheek molded against his shoulder as if by design, and her palms slid up his back. She felt corded muscle and scented dampness from his exertion. The steady sound of his breathing almost completed the sensory package. All that was missing was taste.

He supplied it by tilting her head up and bringing his mouth down to cover hers, breathing in the sigh she had begun to release. The mingling of her breath with his felt so erotic that her heart picked up speed.

The effect increased when he flicked the corner of her mouth with his tongue. She opened her mouth in surprise, probably just as he had intended, and he used the advantage to deepen the kiss.

Her senses spun. Clinging to him to steady herself only intensified the feeling. She had forgotten how well he could play her, like an instrument in which he was a virtuoso.

Even as logic insisted she should end this, part of her returned his kiss with all the pent-up passion inside her. She had no business allowing herself such an indulgence, but she could no more push him away than she could fly.

As he lifted his mouth away, she murmured a protest, then sighed again as he rained tiny kisses along her jaw and down the sensitive column of her throat. He cupped her face, looking at her from under heavy lids as if seeing her for the first time.

"I dreamed of this," he said huskily.

He wasn't dreaming, he was remembering, but she wasn't going to tell him so. He had held her and kissed her more times than she liked to think. With no memory beyond their working relationship, he thought this was the first time his mouth had almost drowned hers in a kiss so sweetly demanding, that she wouldn't have cared if she never surfaced again. He had no idea that they had resisted the pull between them for almost two months, pretending that theirs was a purely professional relationship.

After he'd kissed her on the night of the trade dinner,

she could no longer pretend. Mathiaz had worked his way into a corner of her heart she had walled off since her late teens. He not only ignited her senses in every way possible, he seduced her mind, too. She was skilled in defending herself against physical encroachment, but had no practice at keeping someone like Mathiaz out of her mind.

Her thoughts spun back to candlelit dinners in his villa, as he fascinated, aroused and intrigued her with his conversation, as well as his beguiling touch. One night he had arranged to screen a movie especially for her. Afterward, in the darkness of the private theater, they'd come so close to making love that heat poured through her thinking about it now.

Although she told herself she was relieved that he couldn't remember, she felt stupidly hurt to think that the night he had told her he loved her wasn't burned on his memory the way it was on hers.

The baron had received another threatening letter, this time with a live bullet enclosed in the envelope, hand delivered to his villa. The stalker had known how to bypass the palace security protocols, giving himself away as an insider, The mistake had enabled him to be caught within hours.

She should have left then, but had allowed Mathiaz to convince her to stay, supposedly to help tighten up palace security protocols. They both knew the real reason. He wanted her to stay, so she stayed.

A month after the stalker was caught, Mathiaz had arranged a moonlit picnic in a secluded area of the garden at Château Valmont, instructing palace security to allow them their privacy. The champagne and excellent food, moonlight and the perfume of roses had bewitched her into forgetting that she shouldn't let him kiss her, far less caress her so intimately that her eyes blurred just thinking of that night.

Afterward they had gone for a midnight stroll along the private beach and he had told her that he was in love with her.

He hadn't understood when she pulled away from him in panic. How could he, when she barely understood herself? Like Cinderella fleeing the ball on the stroke of midnight, she'd gone back to her suite in the guest wing, and started packing. Her resignation had been on his desk next morning.

He had asked her to explain, plainly hurt by her apparent change of heart. Her job at the château was done, she informed him, the finality of it echoing in her soul. Time she moved on. She knew she sounded uncaring, when it was the last thing she felt. Better he thought she didn't care, than discover how much she did, when her every instinct rejected the feeling.

She hadn't wanted him to know about the panic attack his declaration of love had brought on, ashamed to admit how the thought of loving anyone paralyzed her. If he knew, he would want more from her than she was capable of giving. So she told herself she was doing the right thing leaving now before she hurt him more than she had already. For herself, it was already too late.

No one else had ever held her so tenderly, or made her feel such intense emotions. She put them into her response now, blindly, hungrily, the long months of deprivation overriding the inner voice that warned her she was playing with fire.

How had she found the strength to walk away from him, and live without him for ten of the longest months of her life? How was she going to find the strength to walk away a second time?

"Jacinta," he murmured, his lips moving against her mouth. "While I was unconscious, I dreamed of you, and this was exactly how I imagined kissing you would feel."

She turned her head away, trying to sound unaffected, when it was the last thing she felt. "In my experience, reality rarely measures up to our dreams."

He dropped his hands to his sides and moved back a few paces. "I wanted to know, all the same."

She kept the disappointment out of her voice. "And now?"

"Now we practice those falls."

She should be glad he had the strength to stop when he did, but regret pulsed through her as she went to the dressing room and changed. Close combat was probably the last exercise she should contemplate with Mathiaz, but since she couldn't risk any other kind of intimacy, she decided to take what comfort she could in this kind.

When she emerged from the dressing room, he was waiting for her at the padded floor area. His loose-fitting white pants and tunic matched hers. The sash around his waist was also black.

"You sure you want to go through with this?" she asked more cheerfully than she felt.

He cocked an eyebrow at her. "Regretting accepting my challenge already? I'll try not to do too much damage."

"I was more concerned about hurting your leg."

"Let me worry about the leg. You worry about surviving."

She was already worried about survival, but knew he didn't mean the same kind she did. Emotional survival worried her more than dealing with his greater physical strength. She was trained to handle opponents twice her size, but her training hadn't included what to do when your opponent kissed you and left your mind so fogged you could hardly think straight.

She forced her mind to clear and bowed ceremonially to him. He returned the bow, then began to circle around her, warming up.

The first couple of times he threw her easily, and let her throw him once out of courtesy. Then she managed to throw him once without his cooperation. She saw the look of surprise on his face as he landed, slapping the mat to absorb the impact of his fall.

Rolling to his feet, he began to react with more strength, demanding more from her to keep up. "You're good at this," he said as she rolled to her feet, after another fall.

"For a woman of my size," she added, tongue firmly in cheek.

"I didn't say that."

"You didn't have to. I'm used to being underestimated."

"I have the feeling I'm doing it now." He sounded as if he meant something more than the friendly bout.

"Are you remembering something?"

He frowned. "Not sure. I have the feeling we've done this before, or something very like it. Have we?"

"This is the first time we've practiced martial arts together," she said with scrupulous honesty.

He circled again, looking for an opening. "But not the first time I've kissed you."

Apprehension prickled along her spine. "You said you dreamed about it. Sometimes the mind can't tell the difference between a real experience and one that's strongly imagined."

"Now you sound like Pascale." Mathiaz said in annoyance, as if her evasiveness bothered him more than her fast footwork.

She was bothered, too, for different reasons. She didn't like lying to him even by omission, but how else could she describe her refusal to tell him what had gone on between them in the year he had lost?

Why didn't she simply tell him that she was the one who couldn't deal with the closeness blossoming between them?

Mathiaz lunged at her with a speed that surprised her, given his injury. When he grasped her and pulled her down to the floor with him, her mind whirled back to when she was eighteen, returning from a date with her first love, the man she had fully expected to marry when they were old enough.

They had blown a tire on a back road on the way home from a dance. She had been helping Colin change the tire when a group of teenagers pulled up beside them, making lewd, drunken comments.

They had ignored the catcalling, but the four drunken youths piled out of the car and encircled her. She had tried talking to them, hoping to defuse the situation, but they began pawing her. When Colin tried to stop them, one of the youths struck him from behind with the tire lever. Colin slumped to the ground. Never had Jacinta felt more helpless.

She tried to reach Colin but two of the men pulled her to the ground. A third dragged her dress up around her waist. Her attempts to kick and bite her assailants proved useless. She knew what would have happened next if a police car hadn't cruised to a halt beside them, lights blazing. After a scuffle, the youths were arrested. She had been vindicated to see them convicted of Colin's murder.

She had made up her mind never to be helpless again, learning every self-defense move she could, and finding that she had an unerring eye with a gun. Perhaps because she now projected an air of being able to take care of herself, she had never needed to use any of her skills other than in practice.

It had taken her a few years to learn that her ability to let anyone get close to her had also been a casualty of that night. After panicking as soon as she began to care too much about anyone, she had made sure her dates weren't allowed to progress beyond friendship.

Until Mathiaz.

She had resisted his appeal as long as she could, telling herself that anything else was unprofessional. He had no such qualms, making his feelings for her plain, as well as ensuring that she knew he didn't give his heart lightly. She had really thought she could respond in kind, until the night when he told her he loved her. Until her sense of panic had become too strong to fight. No amount of logic could shake her terror that if she allowed him to love her, something terrible would happen to him, too.

Caught up in the memory of the attack, she fought Mathiaz as if possessed, almost succeeding in breaking his hold on her until she realized who he was, and where they were. In her confusion, he was able to pin her beneath him. She had no choice but to concede the match.

He looked down at her, enjoying the moment. She tensed, thinking he meant to kiss her again, but instead he smiled in triumph. ''What was that about hurting me?''

She let him give her a hand up, resisting the urge to use the leverage to flip him over her shoulder. One day she would have to warn him about making such a basic mistake. "I always fantasize when I'm fighting, don't you?"

He grinned. "Sure. I fantasize that what we're doing isn't fighting."

She felt her cheeks glow, and looked away. While they were apart, Mathiaz had figured in her fantasies more often than he had any right to do. She felt the familiar swell of panic start, and made an effort to control her breathing. "I need a shower."

Mathiaz watched her go, feeling puzzled. Whoever she had been fighting just now, he'd wager anything that it wasn't him. When he had lunged at her, she had acted exactly as he'd hoped, moving into his attack and trying to throw him off balance. The move had enabled him to pull her to the floor, pinning her beneath him.

That was the moment when she'd left him to fight some demon of her own imagination. He wished he knew what it was.

There was so much about her he didn't know, including why he felt as if he'd kissed her many times before today. He felt a tug of need. She was so fragile and so strong, and the glow of her exertion made her look beautiful.

Holding her in his arms felt right. He couldn't accept that today was the first time. Some part of him had known exactly how she liked to be touched. He crashed one fist into the other in frustration. If only he could force his way through the fog shrouding his memory, he was sure he would find some answers.

He strode to the changing room and stood under a cool shower for a long time, hoping either to stir some memory of the past year, or wash away his need to know. He did neither, and came out chilled to the bone, his leg aching, and his temper heading for boiling point. Dr. Pascale had said Mathiaz's memory of the last months might be gone for good, but fragments of recollection kept tantalizing him, especially when he spent time with Jacinta. So his next step was obvious. He would spend as much time with her as he could.

Chapter Four

Some people never learned, Jacinta thought furiously as she showered and dressed. Bad enough to let him kiss her. Agreeing to practice unarmed combat with him was the height of folly and could only end in one way, with every nerve in her body screaming for more of his touch, and her mind urging her to get as far away from him as she could before something terrible happened to him as it had to Colin.

She should have turned down this assignment, she knew. But when Dr. Pascale had called to tell her that he needed her help to rouse Mathiaz from his coma, she hadn't hesitated, hastening to the baron's bedside like a lovesick adolescent. Her conceit at thinking she was the one person who could bring him back was going to cost her dearly.

She came out into the gymnasium fluffing her hair with her fingers, and stopped short as she saw the baron pacing up and down. He looked furious.

"Why the grim face? You won," she said. "How's the leg?"

His eyes narrowed in suspicion. "Not as sore as it should be. Next time you fight me at full capacity or not at all."

"What makes you think I didn't this time?" she asked innocently.

"You only put your heart into the bout in the last few seconds. I don't know what personal demon you were fighting, but it wasn't me. Who was it, Jacinta?"

She stuffed her sports clothes into her bag, keeping her face averted. "You're imagining things."

His fingers bit into her shoulder as he spun her around to face him. "I've lost a chunk of my memory, not my mind. Now are you going to tell me, or do I fire you and get myself a bodyguard who'll level with me?"

"Perhaps you should get someone else. I'm not really cut out for this."

At her defeated tone, he let his hands drop. "Damn it, Jacinta, I don't want anyone else. I want to know why I feel the way I do around you, when we're supposed to mean nothing to each other."

She made herself meet his eyes. "How *do* you feel around me?"

He combed his dark hair with one hand. "As if I'm being pulled in ten different directions at once. My mind tells me we met a couple of months ago when I hired you to handle a stalker, and that's it. But my body tells a different story. They can't both be true."

"You're confused because of the memory loss. Dr. Pascale said..."

"I know what Pascale said," Mathiaz snapped. "I also know he's a lot more devious than most people give him credit for. If he lured you back to work for me, he had a good reason.''

''Such as?''

''Such as trying to throw us back together because he can't help wanting the whole world paired off two by two.''

She shrugged carefully. ''So he's a romantic beneath that crusty exterior. What does that have to do with us?''

''Exactly. What does it have to do with us?''

She swallowed. ''You're talking in circles. Perhaps the accident...''

''Perhaps nothing. Have you considered that I might have remembered something about the last year?''

She took an involuntary step backward, sure that her face betrayed her shock. If he had remembered that he had said he loved her, and that she had walked out on him, his anger made sense. She opened her mouth to confirm what he already knew, then closed it again. ''Very clever,'' she said softly, alerted barely in time.

His expression remained carved from stone. ''You were about to say?''

''That it's a lovely day outside with a balmy sea breeze blowing, and only a ten percent chance of rain.''

He looked as if he would like to throw her to the mat again and pin her there until she gave him the answers he wanted. He had no way of knowing how close she had just come. Only the puzzlement she saw in his eyes had stopped her. No matter how he pretended, the last year was still a blank to him. If there was any justice in the world, it would stay that way for both their sakes.

''Thanks for the weather report.'' He picked up his stick and headed for the door.

She grabbed her bag. ''Where are we going?''

"*We* aren't going anywhere. I'm going for a walk along the beach."

"Not alone, you're not."

"Didn't I just prove which of us is the stronger?"

She sighed. "Strength has nothing to do with this. If I'm to be your bodyguard, you have to let me do my job."

"You've made your point. Let's get going. You can leave your bag here. The staff will return it to your suite."

He led the way out of the gymnasium and through the trees, along a walkway of crushed coral, down to the private beach that marked one boundary of the royal compound known as Château Valmont.

She checked the beach ahead for signs of an intruder. The sand was as pristine as the receding tide had left it. All the same she stayed alert, her gaze swinging from the shoreline to the trees lining the beach.

She was sure he took deliberately long strides to force her to jog to keep up. The walking stick swung from his hand but he hardly used it for support, she noticed. She debated asking him to lend it to her.

A mile along the beach, when he showed no signs of slowing down, she latched on to his arm. "Dr. Pascale prescribed moderate walking to strengthen your leg. He said nothing about forced marches."

The baron's angry look raked her. "If you can't take the heat..."

She stepped in front of him and planted her fists on her hips. "I can take the heat, all right. I should be used to it after all the times we disagreed over you heading off without me, when I was supposed to be protecting you."

He moved a patch of seaweed around with his foot. "I don't see myself as the argumentative type."

"A lover, not a fighter," she muttered under her breath.

He gave her a sharp look. "What?"

"Nothing. When your former employee started making threats, you accepted the need for extra security, but you didn't like it. So we argued."

His expression softened. "I can't imagine I objected to having you around."

He hadn't, that was the problem. "I'd rather not stand around discussing it. Moving, you make less of a target," she said. She noticed that his gaze was clouded. She guessed the match and the walk were taking a toll. "Are you in pain?"

"I'm fine," he said shortly. "Let's keep walking."

"As long as we head back toward the villa," she insisted. "I knew that workout was too much for you."

He gave a derisive laugh. "Too much for whom? You were the one who ended up conceding the match." But he dropped an arm around her shoulder, casually, as if in friendship. She felt his weight settle on her, and tried not to look too much as if she was helping him.

His arm around her felt entirely too good. She needed every bit of discipline to stop herself from leaning into his embrace. As she breathed in the warm masculine scent of him, mixed with the tang of the sea air, she allowed herself to imagine they were a couple, out for a stroll along the beach.

A sudden tightening in her chest sounded a warning. Too close, too close, her mind screamed. She felt the breath catch in her throat, and made an effort to breathe normally. How could she want something as much as she did Mathiaz's attention, when she couldn't handle it?

The first time she had panicked when she felt herself becoming close to someone, she had gone to the family doctor in Orange County, fearing she was losing her mind. The doctor gave her some reading material about panic attacks, and urged her to see a specialist in the field. She had tried therapy to the point where she no longer felt as if she had to run away every time she felt a surge of affection for a man. But anything stronger, and her mind simply shut down.

She knew why she hadn't told Mathiaz. With him, she had hoped she would react differently. He was considerate, intelligent, everything she admired in a man. At first, her own powerful emotions had overwhelmed her fear, so for a time, she had been able to return his affection without succumbing to panic.

The night he declared his love for her, her fear had been dulled by champagne, and her senses swamped by the strength of her feelings for Mathiaz. Letting him caress her as intimately as a lover had seemed more natural than anything she'd ever done.

It wasn't until she realized he wanted more from her that she had begun to panic. He wanted her to stay, to be a part of his life. He hadn't actually mentioned marriage, but he had intimated that it wouldn't be long. And she wasn't ready.

She would never be ready as long as the thought of entrusting her heart to him filled her with such terror.

Mathiaz stopped walking and she looked up at him. "Is something wrong?"

His gaze looked far away, and he focused on her with an obvious effort. "Walking with you like this triggered something."

Fear clutched at her heart. "A memory?"

"More like a ghost of something, like when you try to recall a name and it dances around the edge of your mind, just out of reach."

"Maybe you shouldn't try to force it." Who was the advice meant to protect, him or herself?

"I didn't." His hold around her shoulders tightened. "I got a glimpse of walking together on this beach some other time."

She injected a teasing note into her voice. "Probably wishful thinking."

"I don't think so. We were happy. Celebrating something, but what?"

Before she could decide how to answer, a flash of something metallic glinted through the trees fringing the beach. She stiffened, sliding out from under Mathiaz's arm to move in front of him. She pitched her voice low. "I think someone's watching us from the trees."

"Palace security?"

"Maybe." The flash worried her. "Walk over to that group of rocks, casually as if it was your intention all along. Don't let him know we've spotted him."

"Him? Damn it, Jacinta, I don't plan on scurrying behind a rock every time you see a deer move through the trees."

"Deer don't carry guns." She didn't know it was a gun for sure, only something metallic, but the warning had the desired effect.

Mathiaz moved to the boulders but kept her hand in his, towing her with him into their shadow. When he pulled her down beside him, she tried to resist but he was stronger. She kept her voice down. "Let me go, I have a job to do."

"Getting yourself killed? If someone is out there and

they're armed, what are you going to do, kick sand in their face?''

''I'm armed, too,'' she told him furiously. ''And I can use it.''

His brow furrowed. ''Have we had this discussion before?''

''You don't want to know.'' Her tone told him that they had.

''Exactly how long did you work for me?''

She sighed. Trapped behind the boulders with him, she could hardly scout the area to confirm what she had glimpsed among the trees. But at least they had cover, so she decided to answer him. ''Four months, from September until December last year.''

He looked dubious. ''Catching the stalker took four months?''

''Three.''

''And the extra month?''

She felt her breath falter. ''You wanted my advice on improving your security arrangements. Maybe you also liked having someone to argue with. Can't we save this discussion? Someone's coming down the beach.''

He released her but his expression told her they would continue their talk later. She only hoped they would have a later. She reached inside her shirt, freeing the compact automatic weapon she carried. She listened to the footfalls coming closer, counted to three, then whirled into a standing position, weapon held in two outstretched hands, using the boulder to steady her aim.

''Hey, what are you doing?''

She felt her heartbeat settle a little as she recognized the baron's equerry, Barrett Lyons, a tall, ascetic-looking man with thinning black hair and watery blue eyes behind thick glasses. She lowered the gun and holstered it. "What are you doing here?"

"Looking for Lord Montravel. The gymnasium staff told me he came this way." The equerry's voice shook, as well it might. He had come within a hair's breadth of getting himself killed.

Lyons had worked for Prince Henry until his death. His long service to the Carramer crown had merited Mathiaz giving Lyons a place on his staff, although the baron didn't much like the man.

Jacinta didn't like him either, since learning that he had provided a reference for Mathiaz's stalker, Andre Zenio. Security had investigated Zenio's background, and substantiated Lyons's claim to have met Zenio while doing charity work and his desire to help the young man improve himself. No other obvious connection between them had come to light. Although Lyons professed shock over his protégé's behavior, Jacinta still felt he knew more than he was telling.

Mathiaz didn't remember hiring Lyons any more than he remembered his uncle's death, so he was grateful to the older man for briefing him about current affairs of state. Now Mathiaz frowned at him. "What was it you wanted, Lyons?"

Lyons looked nervously at Jacinta. "You asked me to remind you that you're seeing the president of Valmont Bank at midday."

He caught Jacinta's frown of disapproval before she could hide it. "Like you, I have my duty," he said.

She had never been able to argue with him when it came to duty. As Valmont's finance minister, and chancellor of the state treasury, his responsibilities were crushing, but he handled them with an ease she envied.

"Dr. Pascale would say you need more time to recover."

"Pascale would have me sitting in a rocking chair, watching the ocean," the baron said scathingly.

"Wouldn't hurt for a few more days."

She knew the battle was lost when Mathiaz began to discuss business with his equerry, heading back toward the compound as they talked. She followed, automatically keeping an eye on the surroundings.

"What were you doing watching us from the trees?" she asked Lyons.

He looked affronted. "I wasn't watching anyone. Dew dripped from a tree onto my glasses. I stopped to polish them."

So much for the flash she had seen. Not gun metal, but the sun glinting off the equerry's bifocals. So why did she feel a prickle of unease along the back of her neck, the seat of her most reliable intuition?

Something was bothering her.

She grew angry with herself. She was working for a man who had been in love with her, but who had no memory of what they had shared. Wasn't that enough to bother anyone? If she had an ounce of professionalism, she would ask the royal protection detail to find a replacement for her. She was too involved. How could she protect Mathiaz properly when every moment spent with him threw her senses into a tailspin?

At the same time she knew that resigning wasn't an option. She cared too much about Mathiaz to trust anyone else with his life. However hard this was, and she suspected it might go all the way to impossible, she was determined to stay at his side until whoever set the explosion was caught. But who would protect her from him?

Chapter Five

Having a workaholic to look after made her job easier, Jacinta thought as she thumbed through a magazine in Mathiaz's outer office where she had positioned herself so she could keep an eye on anyone who approached. The need to do so didn't stop her from being bored out of her mind.

She told herself she should be pleased he spent so much time in his office and the Cabinet Room. He was in no danger from whoever had set the explosives. The only time she needed to worry was when he wanted to go out, and so far, he hadn't seemed keen to leave the royal compound.

Without telling Mathiaz, she had consulted Dr. Pascale, who had assured her that Mathiaz's behavior was understandable for someone coming to terms with amnesia. "Finding out that you've lost a year's worth of memories is unsettling for anyone, but for someone accustomed to being in control, like Mathiaz, it can be especially disturbing," the doctor had said. "Don't be surprised if the baron wants to stay on familiar territory for the time being.''

She looked up as the door opened and Mathiaz emerged. Seeing her curled on the leather couch, he scowled. ''You don't have to stand guard outside my door every minute.''

She saw Barrett Lyons smirk behind his thick glasses. She uncurled and stretched, putting the magazine down. ''Just doing my job.''

She *really* didn't like Mathiaz's assistant, she thought. He had made no secret that he didn't welcome her presence in the outer office which he plainly considered his domain. Tough. She had a job to do the same as he did, and he may as well get used to having her around. With no clues as to who had set the explosives that injured Mathiaz, everyone was under suspicion, including staff who had been with the royal family since the dark ages.

''I told Ms. Newnham that I can notify her if anything untoward happens,'' Lyons said.

''I suppose you can disarm an assailant, too,'' she said. Lyons colored with annoyance.

Mathiaz heard, too. ''Were you two always this combative?''

Lyons sniffed. ''Since I didn't join your staff until after Prince Henry passed away, Lord Montravel, Ms. Newnham and I haven't had a lot to do with each other.'' He sounded as if that was fine with him.

Mathiaz gestured to her. ''Join me in my office, Jacinta.'' When Lyons started to get up, he said, ''I won't need you for the moment, Lyons, thank you. See that we're not disturbed.''

''You really shouldn't needle the man,'' Mathiaz said as he closed the door. The walking stick stood behind it but he used it less and less now. He gestured her to a seat. Instead of returning to his desk, he took a seat beside her and hooked one foot over the other knee with no sign that the posture caused him any discomfort.

She wished she could say the same for herself. His nearness made the breath rise in her throat. "You might give him the same advice, Baron."

"He's old and set in his ways."

"So I'm the one who should make concessions." She sighed. "You're absolutely right. I only wish he didn't remind me of those faithful retainers in old Hollywood horror movies." She let her voice drop to her boots and intoned, "You rang, master?"

Mathiaz smiled, and her insides clenched. Trying to keep her distance worked as long as they weren't in the same room together. When he was within touching distance, she had no hope. She shifted in her seat. "Have you remembered something?"

His eyes darkened. "Bits and pieces, like fragments of a dream."

A tremor gripped her. Was their relationship one of those fragments? "Anything specific?"

He combed his hair with his fingers. "This morning I remembered attending the state funeral for Uncle Henry. At least there's a funeral in my mind, lots of people in dark clothes, and great pomp and ceremony."

Still wary, she forced a smile. "I watched it on television along with most of Carramer." She didn't add that she had watched the telecast hoping to catch a glimpse of Mathiaz. "Sounds like you're making progress."

"Not enough, and too slowly."

As if unable to sit still, he gained his feet and moved to a coffee pot simmering on a side table. "Coffee?"

"Yes, please." Her mouth was dry enough to use for blotting paper.

He handed her a cup. She took it, being careful not to touch his fingers. Her mind was in enough turmoil without that. "Have you remembered anything besides the funeral?"

"This morning I turned on the computer and called up a project I started a couple of months ago, judging by the date on it. I worked on it for a half hour before it dawned on me that I shouldn't be able to remember it. As soon as I started to concentrate, the memory fell apart."

"Which proves the doctor is right, forcing yourself to remember isn't the way to go."

Mathiaz slammed his cup down on the edge of the desk hard enough to wash liquid into the saucer. "The doctor doesn't have to deal with this feeling of emptiness, as if there's a chasm in my mind I can't get across. Everything I need to know is there, if only I could reach it."

She touched a hand to his arm. "I can't possibly understand how you feel, but if it helps, I'm here for you." She had thought the words but hadn't meant to say them until she heard them spill from her lips.

He stood up, took the cup from her hands and set it aside, and pulled her to her feet. "Why do I feel as if you're the bridge that can get me across that chasm?"

Because he had once loved her. Because she cared for him. The thought was enough to make her want to turn and run, but she used all her willpower to stay where she was. Right now he needed her more than she needed to get away.

Could the answer be that simple? she wondered distantly. Could she control her fear of loving too much by focusing on his needs, instead of her own? So far the strategy seemed to be working.

Mathiaz lifted one of her hands to his mouth and kissed the knuckles. "It's a shame you weren't with me through the missing year, or you could tell me what I need to know."

Her fear increased along with a desire so wanton and powerful that it overrode the panic. "Mathiaz, this isn't a good idea."

His gaze warmed. "Right now it feels like a very good idea."

Still keeping her hands in his, he bent his head and kissed her. The desire fanned into flame. "We shouldn't..." she tried again.

The words got lost in his mouth as he worked her lips gently, arousingly, his tongue teasing a response she was powerless to withhold. He moved closer, trapping her hands against his chest so she felt the steady beat of his heart under her fingertips. The beat distracted her from her halfhearted attempt to push him away. His hands slid over her shoulders and her body turned liquid.

"A very good idea," he murmured against her mouth.

She had no words for what she was feeling. The months evaporated and she knew only that she was where she wanted to be, in Mathiaz's arms, her bones melting as his hands skimmed her back.

The air in the room had rarefied. She could hardly breathe. Her thoughts were dazed. She didn't want him to seduce her. Surely once had been enough?

Once could never be enough, she accepted. But twice was a recipe for disaster. She splayed her hands against his chest with more force. "Mathiaz, you don't know what you're doing." Once he remembered that he had declared his love for her, and she had walked out on him, he would be furious with himself for kissing her. No matter how much she enjoyed being in his arms, she owed it to him to keep her distance.

No one said she had to like it.

He released her and walked to the window, staring out. She wondered how much of the expansive view he was seeing. Not much, she gathered from his distracted expression when he turned around. "You tell me I don't know what I'm doing. Yet every instinct tells me having you in my arms is the right thing. Have I kissed you before?"

She felt her cheeks flame. "Yes."

"Have we made love?"

The answer stuck in her throat. Could she call moments of passion when she was pushed to the brink of desire "making love"? "Not exactly."

His eyes brightened, boring into her. "Not exactly making love sounds like being a little bit pregnant. Did we sleep together or not?"

Relief that she could answer truthfully warred with her wish that she didn't have to. "No, we didn't sleep together."

"But we wanted to?"

"Mathiaz, please..."

"Answer the question or you're fired."

She hesitated, wondering whether to call his bluff. "Go ahead and fire me," she said quietly. The thought of leaving swamped her in misery, but anything was better than dealing with this. Mathiaz couldn't know that he was rubbing salt into a raw wound with every word.

He grabbed a chair and spun it around, straddling it like a cowboy. The knuckles he curled around the back were pale, she noticed, wondering if he had put the chair between them as a defense mechanism.

"I wish I could. But as long as you hold the key to the hole in my memory, I'm not letting you go," he said.

She collected the cups from his desk and carried them to the wet bar adjacent to his office. Glad of something to do, she began to wash the delicate china.

"We have servants to do that," he called irritably.

She stayed where she was. "What makes you think I won't leave of my own accord?" she asked through the doorway.

"You didn't have to come back in the first place."

He was right, she didn't. "I wanted to help if I could. You're not in a coma now," she pointed out, drying her hands and wishing she could have found a few more cups to wash.

"I need you, Jacinta."

The softly spoken statement was all it took. She hooked the towel over a gold rail and returned to his office. "Don't," she said around a huge lump clogging her throat.

He stood up and swung the chair back to its previous position beside the desk. "Don't admit to needing you? Why not?"

"You're assuming I feel the same way."

She would have given anything not to have to witness the desolation that invaded his expression. "Are you trying to tell me I fell in love with you, but you didn't return my feelings?"

What was the honest answer? "I told you I wasn't ready," she said carefully.

"Then what did we do?"

"I—left." Two words that didn't nearly explain the bleakness of the ten months she'd endured without him.

Or the hurt she'd inflicted on him when he didn't understand why she had no choice.

"You left, just like that. You're a liar, Jacinta."

His harshly grated accusation speared to her core. "You don't know what you're talking about," she denied wildly.

He came closer, his hands dropping to her shoulders, kneading out the knots she knew his fingers could read in her muscles. "You wouldn't be this tense if you felt nothing for me."

She didn't move away. His touch felt much better than she deserved. "Leaving the first time was hard. I didn't expect to have to do it a second time."

His fingers skimmed around the back of her neck, linking there, holding her although his gaze alone would have pinned her. "Then don't. Let's explore what we can be to each other. We can start again, with everything fresh and new."

"For you." For her, there was too much emotional baggage.

"For you, too. I'll make sure of it."

She spun out of his grasp, panic gripping her. "How can you without wiping my memory clear, too?"

"There is a way."

She found herself on the other side of his desk. Now who was seeking a defense mechanism? Her legs weakened and she dropped into his chair, gripping the edge of the desk with both hands. The chair smelled of aged leather, the desk was littered with documents bearing the royal seal. The details leaped out at her as her thoughts churned. "What are you talking about?"

He leaned across the desk, his face alarmingly close. "I was going through my diary notes covering the missing months. The first two months make especially interesting reading."

Because she figured so largely in them, she guessed. She affected a shrug. "They were difficult months, with the stalker threatening you."

"Zenio hardly rates a mention," he said softly. "But you do."

She swallowed hard. How much detail did his diary go into? Had he been toying with her all this time? If he already knew that she'd walked out on him, why were they having this conversation? Why had he kissed her? To punish her for leaving him without warning or explanation?

She stood up. "Then I guess you know all you need to."

His palm hit the desk with the force of a gunshot, making her jump. "Not by a long shot. All the diary tells me is that we spent a great deal of time together."

"I was your bodyguard. I was expected to go everywhere you went."

"To dinner in my suite? To a private screening of a movie?"

Her heart rate jumped. "We had a few dates."

"More than a few."

She toyed with a gold pen on an elaborate stand. "They were part of my cover."

"I would have thought the cover was needed only when we were in public together."

Her fingers tightened around the pen. "I like to be thorough."

He stepped away from the desk and she could breathe again. "Then you should approve of my plan to re-enact the events in my diary and see where they lead me."

He couldn't be so cruel as to expect her to go through

the whole experience again, only to have things end the same way? Then it came to her that he had no idea what those months had been like for her. "Have you asked Dr. Pascale what he thinks of the idea?"

"He thinks anything that helps restore my memory is a good idea."

She hadn't expected that. "How...how do you go about reliving a lost year?" she asked, heart thumping wildly.

"I can't exactly relive the year, but I can recreate a lot of the events," he explained. "Josquin refuses to give me a full workload while I'm convalescing. He may be my cousin but he's still the Crown Regent and my boss. So I may as well use the time constructively, by recreating the experiences in the diary."

He was going to court her all over again, and he didn't even know it. How could she agree to such torment? "I'm not sure I want to do this," she denied.

His dark gaze challenged her. "Because you don't believe it will work, or you're afraid it might?"

"You know I want to do everything I can to help you."

He heard the unevenness in her voice. "I won't command you to do this."

She almost wished he would. Her democratic instincts would rebel against any attempt at royal command. She might even manage to break free, and wondered if he knew. "No fair, Baron," she muttered. "No wonder your people keep voting to retain the monarchy. You give them enough freedom so they don't feel compelled to rise up and overthrow you."

He settled one thigh on the edge of the desk, letting the other leg swing free. "Their freedom isn't an illusion, any more than yours is. Did you quit my service last time because you felt you lacked freedom?"

She struggled against the pulse fluttering in her throat. "I never felt restricted working for you." Her panic had come from inside her. Mathiaz had only been the cause.

He nodded. "You're not restricted now. Whatever was between us must have been mutual, or you wouldn't have chosen to come back."

He had no idea how mutual, she thought, letting her eyes close. She opened them again resolutely. According to the old saying, if you didn't learn from history, you were doomed to repeat it. Could she learn from her history, ensuring that this time, things worked out differently between herself and the baron? "Your idea might work," she said.

Suspicion clouded his gaze as he watched her. "Your capitulation is rather sudden, isn't it?"

She returned his look as openly as she could, although her heart was pounding. What she was considering bordered on insanity. But she was committed. "I'm merely agreeing with your plan. Where do you want to start?"

He looked as if he wanted to say more, but evidently decided to accept her agreement at face value. For now, anyway. "The last thing I recall clearly is visiting Uncle Henry, then the state funeral. After that, only fragments."

He reached across his desk, retrieving a leather bound volume with the year incised in gold on the front. "According to my diary, we attended a reception for the Australasian trade delegation together. Do you recall the occasion?"

How could she forget the first time he had kissed her, she thought, feeling a flutter of dismay. She suppressed the sensation. She could do this. "I remember it."

"Rubber chicken and boring speeches," he said, startling her.

"You remember?"

He gave a hollow laugh. "I remember dozens of similar occasions, and your reaction tells me this one was no different from the others."

She inclined her head in acknowledgment. "The head of the delegation *was* pretty boring."

"Where was the dinner held?"

"At the Royal Yacht Club in Perla."

"And afterward?"

Afterward, they had driven along the coast in his limousine, stopping to admire the play of moonlight on the water while they talked into the night. Did an omission count as a lie? "We returned to the château. You went to bed."

"Alone?"

Something in his tone made her look up. The desire she saw in his gaze almost stopped her heart. "Yes, alone."

His sigh was tinged with regret. "Then I won't gain much from replaying that night." He flipped through gilt-edges pages. "This could be more helpful. Evidently I arranged a private screening of a movie, *Moonlight.* Do you recall anything about the guest list?"

"You mean other than you and me?"

His eyebrow arched. "The screening was for the two of us?"

"It was my birthday," she said in reluctant explanation.

He closed the book with a thump. "Then we'll start with the movie screening."

"But it isn't my birthday."

He thought for a moment. "We'll celebrate my survival. And your return."

Her skin grew hot. The screening of the movie had been their first real date. Her body quivered as she imagined reliving the experience. Could she ensure that the outcome changed this time? She had to, she resolved. She lifted her head. "Very well, we'll celebrate your survival."

"And your return to me."

How could she return when part of her had never really left? "That's unimportant."

He slid off the desk and came around to her side, lifting her chin. "Not from where I stand. I may not remember what we were to each other, but some part of me does. That part keeps insisting that you belong at my side."

"Ever heard of wishful thinking?" she threw at him, unnerved by his light touch on her chin. She wanted to twist free but lacked the will.

He caressed her throat, coming to rest on her racing pulse. "Perhaps it is wishful thinking. Or a deeper knowing. The way I picked up that project this morning suggests my body retains memories that are lost to my mind for the moment. I intend to recapture them, and when I do..."

He would recapture her, she read his unstated intention. She wondered why she didn't simply get up from the chair, walk through the door and keep going. Was there also a part of her that wanted to belong at his side?

No, the denial was almost wrenched from her until she choked it back. For the sake of her own survival, she had to change the outcome this time. She only hoped she was strong enough.

Chapter Six

Everything was going to be different. By next evening she had almost convinced herself. Some things already were. This time he hadn't taken her driving by moonlight or kissed her in the back of a limousine, before arranging the private screening.

Instead he had kissed her in the gym and again in his office. Maybe history wasn't so easily changed after all.

Time she took control. She reached for her clothes. Unable to convince Mathiaz that she didn't need servants, she had allowed the maid to set out her clothes for her, but drew the line at having someone help her dress.

With their reminder of the night Colin was killed, she rarely felt comfortable wearing long dresses, preferring evening pants. These were loose and flowing in black crepe, the pleats falling from a narrow waistband threaded with fine gold chain. She zipped the pants up over her hips and reached for the shimmering gold shell she normally wore with them.

Her hand froze as recognition rocked her. She was certain she had worn the exact same outfit last time. Angrily she hurled the clothing against a wall. She *would* change history.

By the time she was ready to join Mathiaz, she was wearing a lilac chiffon halter top over the evening pants, the scarf neckline hugging her throat and the ends trailing over her shoulders. Too romantic and too revealing, but better than the déjà vu she had experienced with the original outfit.

Mathiaz's eyes lit with appreciation when he saw her. "You look lovely tonight."

"So do you." He looked good enough to eat in dark pants that hugged his muscular legs, and a collarless white shirt, the full sleeves almost medieval. The look suited him, bringing a fluttering sensation into her stomach. She pushed it away. "I hope you have popcorn."

He looked surprised. "For dinner?"

She started to tell him they had shared a late supper last time, not dinner, then stopped herself. The more things they did differently, the more chance she had of changing the outcome. Her impulses were already threatening to get out of hand at the mere sight of him. Putting the width of a table between them sounded like a sensible idea.

Until she saw the table.

He led her outside on to the terrace where servants fussed over the setting. Snowy linen napery, gleaming silverware, candles. Were they real roses strewn over the cloth? Her appreciative nose told her they were. Apart from the halo of candlelight around the table, the rest of the terrace was in shadow. The scene looked disturbingly intimate.

"I thought you'd enjoy eating outside," he murmured at her shoulder.

Her pulse raced. "It's a beautiful night."

"And I prefer late movies."

So did she. For once she was grateful for the presence of the servants. Mathiaz's breath against the back of her neck eroded her determination to change the outcome of the evening. She was not going to let him seduce her this time, but the floaty way she felt made her wonder how much letting would be required.

A butler steered a heated trolley on to the terrace. Wonderful aromas drifted from it, mingling with the scent of roses. "We'll serve ourselves, thank you," the baron told the staff. They bowed their way out, and she and Mathiaz were alone.

He removed a bottle from a silver ice bucket standing beside the table. "Champagne?"

Technically she wasn't on duty, although her instincts were never truly off duty around the baron. Could she make this work by thinking of Mathiaz strictly as a client? Anything was worth a try.

"Only half a glass, thanks," she said.

The pop of a cork was followed by the clink of crystal and the fizz of wine being poured. They were jumping distance from the ground, she assessed, leaning over the marble parapet. Lush lawns sloped away from the terrace to a line of trees silhouetted against the sky. Barely a trace of breeze stirred the branches. The night was still enough for her to hear the restless ocean beyond them.

He came up behind her. "Looking for something?"

She fought the urge to tense. "Habit."

"Any movement you see out there is likely to be the royal security detail." He held out a glass to her.

She took it unsteadily. "I know."

"So there's no reason you can't relax and enjoy yourself." He raised his glass, inviting her to join him, his smile teasing. "This is called a toast. You raise your glass like so, and drink to—what shall we drink to?"

She imitated his gesture, knowing what she would have liked to drink to. Since it wasn't going to happen, she said, "Survival sounds like a good idea."

His mouth curved more deeply. "Too negative. I prefer 'to beauty.'"

He looked into her eyes as he said the words and she felt the blood rush to her head. She hadn't even tasted the champagne and already she felt giddy. She let him drink the toast alone, then murmured, "To destiny," before taking a cautious sip.

His eyes darkened with interest. "Why destiny?"

"Irony. I don't believe in it." When she was a teenager, well-meaning friends had tried to tell her that Colin's death was destiny, that she couldn't have done anything to change the outcome. She had to believe they were wrong. Patterns could be changed. Tonight's pattern had to be.

He steadied the crystal goblet on the wide white parapet and rested his forearms beside it, his face in shadow as he looked out into the night. "What do you believe in, Jacinta?"

"Call me Jac, everyone does." Another small change she could make.

He turned slightly. "I'm not everyone, and Jacinta is such a beautiful name."

She gave a slight shudder, knowing the discussion wasn't the cause. The baron's gaze was too searching for comfort. "Too feminine."

"Have you looked at yourself lately?"

She shifted uncomfortably. "I do know I'm female, if that's what you're saying."

"But you don't like being reminded of it. Why not?"

She took refuge in fact. "As your bodyguard pro tem, I doubt if femininity is an asset. I've been told that male clients sometimes regard a female bodyguard as extremely convenient."

He massaged the back of his neck as if at a painful memory. "Anyone who's gone a round with you in the gym would never make that mistake."

The baron never had. The mistakes had been on her side. "It doesn't hurt to be on my guard," she observed tautly.

Mathiaz straightened. "And you think I'm like that?"

Fairness made her shake her head. "I know you're not."

"I'm glad," he said with quiet determination. "I would never take advantage of our relationship, Jacinta—Jac. I may not remember what passed between us before, but I know myself. I would never take anything you didn't offer willingly."

"You didn't," she said so softly that she wasn't sure she'd spoken out loud.

He heard anyway and took the glass from her hand, setting it down beside his. Her body quivered as he took her in his arms and pulled her into the shadows where they wouldn't be observed. He was so gentle that she wanted to cry, although she almost never cried. The need intensified when his lips skimmed her bare shoulder. She arched her head back.

His mouth moved to her exposed throat. Heat flowed through her. "We shouldn't rush this. Shouldn't we eat something while it's hot?" she said huskily.

"I am."

She felt his hand come around her shoulders and dip into the keyhole opening below the collar of her blouse. His palm felt fiery against her skin as he began a slow massaging movement that sent her pulse rate into orbit.

Almost of their own accord her fingers threaded into his hair, and she pulled his head down against her. His teeth nipped her shoulder and she gasped, then his tongue flickered out to soothe the love bite. Her senses went haywire.

He flicked the scarf ends back over her shoulders, and tugged at the high collar of her blouse. "This floaty material could drive a man crazy. How do you get into this thing?"

"There's a hidden zipper."

He gave a throaty chuckle. "And it's up to me to find it, right?"

She could have stopped him or moved away, but she did neither. Her bones turned to water as he found his own solution to the access problem by sliding his hand along her bare midriff under the blouse. A firestorm of sensation tore through her as his palm trailed up her rib cage, then coasted along the side of her breast. When he cupped her soft fullness, she teetered on the edge of the abyss.

She thought it insane that she allowed him so much, but arched her back to press herself deeper into his hand. The pleasure of having him touch her threatened to undermine her careful plan.

"Was this what happened last time?" he asked, sounding as if his self-control hung by a thread.

She knew hers did. "Something like this," she said on a sharply indrawn breath as he began to caress her other breast.

He pushed the chiffon higher so he could lower his

mouth to her breasts, his kiss scorching. "Then we're doing exactly the right thing."

The only thing she was capable of doing, she thought as fire banked deep inside her. What had happened to her best laid plans? "You don't have to sound so pleased about it," she gasped, clasping his shoulders. She should end this now, but she didn't seem to have the strength.

"Oh, but I am." He looked insufferably pleased, too, when he lifted his head to look deep into her eyes. "I think you are, too."

She could only murmur agreement, knowing no force on earth could have torn her from his arms at that moment. So much for changing history.

He gave a heartfelt sigh. "Unfortunately I agree with you that we shouldn't rush this."

Why had she said such a stupid thing? She almost whimpered when he stepped away from her and adjusted her blouse. She wanted to rip it off altogether and offer herself as an altar for his continued worship. In turn, she would explore him with her hands and her greedy mouth, and they would know paradise.

What was she doing? This was the way the world ended last time. Was there no way off the merry-go-round after all? Slowly she became aware that she had stopped looking for a way off. She felt a soul-deep yearning, but no fear. Where was the urge to run away as far and fast as she could? She could hardly believe it meant there was a chance for them. More likely that his kisses had overwhelmed her fear for the moment. She had no doubt the panic would return. It always had.

Mathiaz retrieved her champagne glass from the parapet. She took it shakily and drank. Dutch courage wasn't the answer but she needed all the help she could get. The fingers he curled around the stem of his goblet weren't entirely steady, either, she noticed with some comfort.

"Was this the mistake I made last time?" he asked, catching her off balance.

"You think kissing me was a *mistake?*"

He heard the hurt in her voice, and shook his head in determined negation. "Of course not. Holding you feels more right than anything I've done since I woke up in the hospital."

She made herself meet his gaze over the rim of the glass. "Then what?"

He put the glass down and skidded a hand over his forehead, pushing his hair back. "I think I rushed you before, and managed to scare you away."

"That's ridiculous." And far too close to the truth for her peace of mind.

"Perhaps, but I'm willing to trust my instinct. All I ask is for you to trust yours, Jac. Trust that I won't do anything to hurt you."

She already trusted him. That wasn't the problem. She felt as aroused as she had ever done, yet she hadn't turned and run. In some distant corner of her mind she had wanted to, but she hadn't. A small victory was still a victory, she told herself.

Mathiaz's decision to go slowly *was* a change. What else might turn out differently, given half a chance? She was almost afraid to hope.

"Let's have dinner," he said, sounding as if he'd far rather continue as they were.

He held a chair out for her and she sat down, then he flicked a white napkin over her lap. Candlelight danced over his features, carving them into fascinating lines. Her hand drifted up to touch his cheek before she realized what she was doing and stopped herself.

He steered the trolley closer and lifted the gleaming covers one by one to show her the delicacies under them. "I didn't know what you'd like, so I had the cook prepare a variety of dishes."

She could see chicken simmering in a sauce so fragrant that it made her mouth water, succulent lobster tails, beef in wine, and several unfamiliar fish dishes. "I'd like to try a little of everything."

"Good idea." He serve them both skillfully, making her wonder where he had learned the art, since he would have grown up being waited on by servants.

When she made the observation, he grinned. "When we were boys, Eduard and I and our cousin, Josquin, used to sneak into the palace kitchens and watch the cooks working. I told my father I was going to be a chef when I grew up."

She laughed at the ordinariness of the memory. "What did he say?"

"He nearly had a fit. He lectured me for an hour on the duties and responsibilities of being royal."

She sampled some of the lobster which melted in her mouth. "I never thought of your royal birth as limiting your options."

"In many ways it does. In others, we have opportunities we wouldn't otherwise enjoy. I've driven a tank, steered an aircraft carrier at sea, shook hands with Michael Jackson."

She felt her eyes widen. "Really?"

He nodded. "He starred at a benefit for a charity I support."

She named some other celebrities most people would give their eyeteeth to meet, and he nodded at them all. Yet he couldn't go into a kitchen and make a sandwich without raising eyebrows. Swings and roundabouts, she told herself. Her life may have been less glamorous, but she had more freedom than he did. And she wasn't the one needing a bodyguard.

The thought was a sobering reminder of their relationship, and she pulled her thoughts back to her plan. So far, the details of their evening had changed, but nothing else. He had still kissed her and set her senses on fire. She still wanted him more than was wise. She tried giving her attention to the food but her senses were so heightened that she was aware of him no matter what she did.

She gave up and set her cutlery down. "Would you like something else? Some dessert?" he asked.

She knew exactly what she would like, and if she confessed, she had no doubt he would oblige her. But that wasn't the answer. She shook her head. "I've had plenty, thank you. The food was excellent."

"Shall I have the staff run the movie now?"

Changes, she reminded herself. "I'm rather tired. I think I'll call it a night."

"Did we get to see the movie last time?"

Not a lot of it, although they had sat in front of the screen to the end, she recalled, feeling flustered as she remembered exactly how they had passed the time. "Every scene," she said carefully.

His dark gaze mirrored his frustration. "I wish I could remember."

She was glad he couldn't. He would only want to take up where they had left off, and she wasn't ready. Would she ever truly be ready? Or would she react as she had done before, by running away?

"I can tell you the plot if you like," she offered.

He shot her a dubious look. "I've a good mind to let you, just to find out if you're bluffing."

"Why would I do that?"

His fingers tightened around the stem of his wineglass. "Because I seriously doubt whether I could sit in the dark with you, and actually see what's on the screen."

Her heart fluttered. "You have a lively imagination."

"You could simply tell me what happened and I wouldn't have to resort to imagination."

She shook her head. "I already did. You refuse to believe me."

"I don't think it's the whole truth." His features took on a look of dread. "Good grief, Jac, tell me I didn't try to force myself on you."

She ground her damp palms together, gaining a glimpse of the horror he was enduring, with the last year a complete blank. "You already said you know yourself better than that."

"That's the trouble, I don't *know*. I think I'm not the kind of man who takes advantage of a woman, and my memories before the explosion support that. But when I'm with you, I feel driven to act like a wild man. I want you, Jac. The feeling is too strong for me not to have felt this way before. I don't like to think it might have affected how I treated you, but your reluctance to discuss it makes me wonder."

She began to fold the napkin with slow precision, averting her gaze. "You didn't do anything you need to apologize for," she insisted, pleating the linen into delicate folds. "Neither of us did."

She looked up. His relief was palpable. "Thank goodness. For a while there, I thought..."

She didn't find out what else he thought, because her attention was captured by a slight movement underneath the balcony. If it had been someone from the royal protection detail, they would have shown themselves. Her senses snapping instantly alert, she pushed away from the table. ''Go back inside and kill the room lights,'' she told Mathiaz in a low voice.

For once he didn't argue. He crossed the marble expanse in long strides and plunged through the wide French doors. She saw him sweep his hand across the light switch and the room beyond the terrace went dark.

The flickering candles lit her way to the parapet and she vaulted over it, hoping she had accurately assessed the distance to the ground. The drop was a fraction longer than she expected and she hit the ground hard. Winded but unhurt, she rolled to her feet.

The sound had come from the bushes to the right of the terrace. She dived into them, colliding with something solid. She felt the heat of a body, heard swearing in a Carramer dialect, then she was slammed viciously against a wall. White pain pulsed through her but she shook it off and lunged at her assailant.

She caught him with a knee to the ribs and reached for his throat, but she was felled by the smash of an arm across her windpipe that brought her to her knees, choking.

She could see the man's outline against the night sky and she rolled, trying to scissor her legs to cut his legs out from under him. But he was quicker and his night vision was better adjusted than hers. He dodged her assault and came back to clamp his hands around her neck, catching the flying ends of the chiffon scarf and twisting them in front of her in a swift movement. She had only a second to wish she had worn the gold shell after all, before her vision began to fade. Her struggles weakened as she tried and failed to drag in fresh oxygen.

Through the gathering haze she heard the sound of a heavy landing and a grunt of pain. Not her assailant because the pressure around her neck didn't slacken. Mathiaz then, jumping off the balcony. Fool, she thought as time seemed to freeze. His injured leg wasn't up to that kind of strain.

The thought that the baron might wade into the fight when he wasn't sufficiently recovered gave her the strength to throw off her assailant. Blessed air rushed into her lungs and the stars receded from her vision. Before she could launch herself at the intruder, he was grabbed from behind and dragged out of the shadow of the building. Moonlight glinted off his face.

Sudden recognition hit her. She knew this man.

The man kicked out at Mathiaz's bad leg, desperation lending him extra strength. Mathiaz went down as if felled, and the intruder tore across the lawn to lose himself among the trees.

She struggled to her feet. "Did you call security?"

Mathiaz nodded, struggling to his feet. "On their way."

No point going after the intruder herself. The guards and the palace dogs would have a better chance of catching up with the man in the dark. "How in blazes did he get in here without triggering an alarm or alerting the dogs?" she demanded, surprised when her abused vocal cords obeyed her.

"I don't know."

She went to Mathiaz, who was massaging his calf. "I'm fine," he insisted when she bent to check. He straightened. "What about you?"

"Fine, too," she insisted, glad he couldn't see her face. She could feel bruising starting to blossom around her neck where the intruder had used her scarf as a garrotte.

She heard barking and saw figures moving toward the

beach, heard someone call out something about the suspect getting into a boat. They'd lost him. She turned her frustration against Mathiaz. "What the devil do you think you were doing?"

"He might have killed you."

"And I might have killed him. Who knows what new damage you've done to your leg leaping off the terrace like that."

"My leg's okay," he insisted. "Your neck is another matter."

"My neck's okay," she parroted him.

"In that case I might have to wring it for you. Your job description doesn't include risking it quite so literally."

She shrugged although the gesture was wasted in the dim light. "That's my job."

"You're working for me. I define your job."

She looked around nervously, seeing lights snap on all over the château and grounds. She heard voices and saw people leaning out of windows. They sounded curious or concerned, or both. "Would you mind defining it inside?"

He understood her concern. "The intruder has gone, or the dogs would be onto him."

They hadn't sounded the alarm before, she thought. There was only one way to get Mathiaz out of danger. She swayed, not sure how much she was acting.

As he supported her his body heat radiated through her and she set her jaw against the temptation to lean into his embrace. Lost in the heat of passion once tonight, she had placed his life in danger. She wasn't going to make the same mistake twice.

She felt herself start to shake. This was Colin all over again. Worse because the man was Mathiaz, and she felt so much more for him than a teenager could ever imagine.

"Shock is catching up with you," he said, misreading her tremors.

She let him hustle her up a set of marble stairs and along a corridor to the room she had left moments before. It felt like hours. She blinked in dismay. The room was full of people all talking at once in a confusing mixture of Carramer and English. They rushed to Mathiaz, but he waved them away and they cleared a path so he could help her to a couch.

She sat, aware that her legs were barely holding her. So much for pretending to need Mathiaz's help. In the bright room lights, he looked better than she felt. Seeing the twisted chiffon at her throat, he peeled it back and gave a low growl of anger. "Somebody call the doctor, on the double."

The barked command snapped her out of the hovering shock. She pushed his hands away. "They're only bruises. No need to send for the cavalry. I'm supposed to *be* the cavalry, remember?"

"How can I? I have amnesia," he snapped back.

She managed to raise an eyebrow. "Convenient."

"And I *am* your client."

She felt too weary to object, knowing he was right anyway. She had to start thinking of him strictly as her client, and not as a man she could love. Tonight she had allowed herself to forget, and the price could easily have been Mathiaz's life.

Chapter Seven

"What do you..." she coughed and tried again, less huskily, "What do you mean, Andre Zenio has a water-tight alibi?"

A day and a half had passed since she and Mathiaz tackled the intruder. Under orders from Dr. Pascale, they were both on light duties until he gave them a clean bill of health. She'd protested that she was perfectly all right, but the bruises on her throat looked like a bizarre necklace of blue, black and yellow. Mathiaz was limping again. For that alone, she wanted to beat Zenio to a pulp. The man had been jailed once for stalking the baron. She couldn't believe he was stupid enough to try it again, but she couldn't deny the evidence of her eyes.

Being confined indoors with Mathiaz meant fighting an even harder battle with herself not to give in to her feelings for him. Dr. Pascale had put the gym off-limits for the time being, so she couldn't punch her way out of the dilemma.

She herself had vetoed the compound's private beach

as too exposed until the intruder was caught. That left the indoor pool and sauna, where they were now. Swathed in a towel, she hunched on a lower bench while Mathiaz did the macho thing on the higher one. Madness to be alone in a cedar-scented cabin with him, wearing only towels. When he had suggested the sauna, she had almost refused, but her will had deserted her. Now she knew she couldn't blame her soaring temperature and racing heart solely on the effects of the sauna.

"I got the call just before we came in here. The police and palace security interviewed Zenio, but he was at the hospital all that night while his wife was having their first baby," Mathiaz explained.

Her exasperation grew. "How could he have a new baby? Nine months ago, Zenio was in jail."

"According to the police, he was a model prisoner so he was allowed to go home for a weekend on compassionate grounds, when his grandmother was seriously ill."

She gritted her teeth. "I know what I saw. It was him."

Mathiaz swung his legs over the edge of the bench and dropped down to her level. "In the shadow of the building, you could have been mistaken."

"When you dragged him off me, his face was in moonlight for a couple of seconds. I'm not likely to forget him after the last time."

The baron's face creased into a frown. "In the heat of the struggle, I didn't get a look at his face at all, so I can't tell you whether it was Zenio or not."

She folded her arms over her towel. "It was. Somehow, he left the hospital during the labor, and broke into the royal compound."

"Hard to believe a man would do such a thing while his baby was being born."

Mathiaz never would, she knew, squirming at the image that sprang to her mind of her having their child, and Mathiaz holding her hand throughout the experience. "Not impossible." The words caught in her throat. Was she talking about Zenio, or herself?

Mathiaz shook his head. "Several staff at the hospital swear that Zenio didn't leave his wife's side all night. Dr. Pascale also saw him there."

"What was the doctor doing at the hospital during the night? He's supposed to be retired." Pascale's idea of retirement differed from hers, she'd already noticed.

Mathiaz hitched his good leg onto the bench, and angled his back against the wall of the sauna. The pose was so relaxed and so masculine that her stomach fluttered. She tried not to notice how little of him the towel covered.

Annoyed with herself, she leaned over and spooned water from a wooden bucket onto a brazier filled with hot coals. They spat and sizzled, and steam rose around her. She breathed shallowly to reduce the searing effect on her lungs.

The baron looked at her through the cloud. "He was visiting a friend who was having a serious operation the next day."

"Hardly visiting hours."

His eyebrow lifted. "Would you like to tell Pascale that?"

She'd already tried telling the doctor his job, and discovered what a bad idea it was. "Probably not."

"I've known Alain Pascale all my life, and he's never misled me about anything. When Eduard and I were kids, if a shot was going to hurt, he never told us it wouldn't."

"Some bedside manner," she sniffed.

"Not textbook, but it taught us we could trust him. If he saw Zenio at the hospital, that's where he was."

She wished Mathiaz had stayed on the upper bench. With him only an arm's reach away, his towel barely covering his magnificent body, she was finding it hard to think straight, let alone focus on the mystery. "Then Zenio has a double," she said.

She stood up, grabbing her towel as it threatened to fall. "I'm going to see if the police have some mug shots I can look at." Anything was better than sitting beside Mathiaz, knowing she couldn't do a thing about the attraction eating her up from inside.

The baron sat up. "You're not going anywhere until you get medical clearance."

She lifted her chin. "You may be under Pascale's authority, but I'm not."

"You are under mine." He made the observation so softly that she wasn't sure she'd heard correctly until she saw his mouth tighten.

She felt a frown start. "Heck of a time to pull rank, Baron."

"All the same, I'm pulling it. If I have to take things easy on doctor's orders, you're going to keep me company."

The very thing she was most afraid of doing. "If I mutiny, do you have a dungeon you can slap me into?"

"I'll think of a suitable penalty. Sit down, please?"

She stayed where she was and gestured with her free hand, recognizing the source of his annoyance. "I thought you were taking Doctor Pascale's restrictions a little too well. The Mathiaz I used to know would have been climbing the walls by now."

He looked rueful, telling her she was on the right track. "You haven't heard how loudly I've complained to Josquin. My dear cousin may be Crown Regent of Valmont Province, but he can't seem to understand that a damaged leg doesn't stop me from using my brain."

"Looks as if we're both stuck for the time being." She had heard Josquin threaten to post a guard outside Mathiaz's office unless she agreed to stay out of it.

He gave an easy smile. "Confinement is much easier to take if you're in the right company."

The walls seemed to close in on her. "I'm not the right company," she denied. "I'm your bodyguard, and not much of one at that."

Mathiaz uncoiled from the bench and came closer. Heat radiated from him. "I won't let you blame yourself for what happened. If anyone's to blame, it's the royal protection detail. One of them could be in league with the prowler."

Her nervousness grew, and she knew better than to blame it on the discussion. "What about the staff who set up the movie projector and arranged the dinner? Secrets are hard to keep in a place this size."

He hadn't considered the staff, she saw in the sudden darkening of his gaze. He was so used to having them around that most of the time he hardly noticed their comings and goings. He stroked his chin thoughtfully. "You have a point. The police are looking at this as an inside job."

She'd never looked at it any other way, and was glad to hear that the police agreed with her. "It would explain how the intruder got past the patrols."

"If they came from *inside*..." he grabbed her hands

and planted a kiss on her damp forehead. "My mind really can't be in gear or I'd have thought of that from the beginning."

She fought the urge to tear her hands out of his. Too close, too close. She had been doing so well, almost able to handle her feelings. Foolishly she had started to hope she might have a future with Mathiaz, until she saw him felled by the intruder. Now the familiar fears were back in full force, reminding her that there was no place for love in her life.

He felt her tug of resistance, and his hold tightened. "What is it, Jac? For a moment, you looked frightened. Of the intruder?"

"Yes."

"I'd hate to think you were frightened of me."

Not of him, of her own response to him, she thought wildly. With his strong fingers curled around hers, she felt trapped, with nowhere to go except the one place she couldn't consider, into his arms. "My towel is slipping," she said, glad it was the truth.

"Can't say I mind." But he released her, and adjusted the folds for her, his touch confident as he tucked the towel more securely around her. She wished she felt as sure of herself.

The moment his fingers connected with her, panic erupted inside her. He smelled of heat and maleness. Tiny droplets of moisture beaded his skin. Awareness of every detail of him slammed through her in an instant, bittersweet because she could do nothing to subdue the fear his touch brought. She cursed the phobia that put him forever beyond her reach.

She saw his face take on a strange, preoccupied look. "A butterfly," he said suddenly.

Some of her panic receded as she assessed his confusion. She touched his cheek. He felt chilled in spite of the sauna's heat, his eyes looking into some distance in his mind.

"Are you remembering something?"

His voice came to her as if from a long way away. "You and I were together on the beach. We'd been swimming. The sea was cold. We came in here to warm up."

"We both enjoyed an occasional sauna, sometimes together," she said tightly, not liking the way her lungs emptied of air suddenly. "It doesn't have to signify anything."

His hands dropped to her shoulders, his fingers digging into the tender flesh. He didn't seem to notice, or hear her. "You looked beautiful, clad only in a suntan and a minuscule towel, much as you are now." His mouth softened. "I tried to persuade you that you didn't need the towel."

She pressed her knuckles against her mouth, well aware of what was coming next, and also that there was nothing she could do to stop the memory.

His smile became a grin of mischief. "We played a childish tug-of-war. The towel came loose—you were clutching it in front of you, and you spun away from me, turning your back. That's when I saw the butterfly."

Of all the details he had to remember, why did it have to be that one? she thought, as angry at herself as with him. She should have known the sauna was a bad idea. "You're dreaming," she snapped.

He came back to her slowly. The half-aware smile vanished and he regarded her seriously. "There's one way to find out." He reached for the towel again.

She took a step backward and almost bumped into the brazier but the wave of heat emanating from it stopped her. Mathiaz stood between her and the door. With nowhere else to go, she could only stand her ground, defiantly clutching the towel. ''If you think I'm going to show you my butterfly, you've got another think coming, Baron.''

Too late she realized she'd betrayed herself, as she saw his gaze lighten. ''So there *is* a butterfly,'' he drawled. ''For a second, you had me convinced it was a fantasy rather than a memory.'' The corners of his mouth tilted up. ''A very attractive memory.''

''I got rid of it,'' she tried.

His expression didn't change. ''I hope they did a neat job. Can't have been easy, removing a tattoo from your...''

''I know where it is...was.'' The sauna's heat wasn't responsible for the color she felt pouring into her face.

He held his right hand up, joining the thumb and index finger to make an oval. ''A Ulysses butterfly if I'm not mistaken. Vivid blue wings, the whole thing about so big. You never did tell me why you got yourself a tattoo.''

She subsided on to the bench. She remembered only too well when she'd had the butterfly done, and why. After Colin's death, she had drifted aimlessly, not sure what she wanted to do next, or if anything was worth doing at all, when it could all be taken away in an instant.

She had been sitting on the verandah of her parents' berry farm, and had noticed an insect struggling to free itself from an ugly cocoon hanging from one of the posts. As she watched, the creature had gradually emerged and revealed itself as a beautiful butterfly. The sight had sent a strong message to her. She could allow her experience to hold her in thrall, or she could fight her way out and transform her life. Getting the tattoo done had been her way of making sure she didn't forget the lesson.

She gave a shrug. "It was a teenage thing. Lots of girls get tattoos on their tush."

"Maybe so, but I get the feeling there's more to it than you're telling me."

She shifted uncomfortably. Why didn't she tell him the whole story and be done with it? More déjà vu, she thought. She had been ready to open up to him when he courted her the last time. Then the fear had come and with it, the compulsion to withdraw, not to allow him to get too close.

She felt the grip of it now. "I can make something up if you like," she offered, her breathlessness belying the light tone.

He looked angry. "Don't bother. If you won't give me the truth, I'd rather you say nothing at all."

His tone lashed her. She looked away. "We had this conversation last time, too."

He dropped to a knee beside her, taking her hands. "Jac, I'm sorry. I couldn't stop the memory, and it felt like something good. If it wasn't..."

His grip steadied her, but she wanted more. She kept her fingers limp in his, afraid that if she followed her inclination, she would pull his head against her breast. "The memory was fine. I'm the one with the problem," she said on a sigh. She forced herself to smile. "We should be celebrating that you remembered something."

His forehead creased into a frown. "For all the good it's doing. All I've done so far is annoy myself and upset you."

"You haven't," she assured him. She had done most of it all by herself. "Have you forgotten this is a sauna?

I don't know about you, but I was cooked about fifteen minutes ago.''

He stood up, keeping her hands in his so she followed him. ''You are turning an interesting shade of scarlet.''

She met his gaze squarely. ''Takes one to know one. Race you to the showers, unless your leg isn't up to it.''

He looked affronted, forgetting their discussion, as she had intended. ''I can still leave you in my wake.''

''We'll see who gets left in whose wake.''

She pushed past him and was well on her way to the showers before she heard him strolling after her, very obviously taking his sweet time. She spun around, feeling her eyes blaze. ''You did that on purpose.''

''The race was your idea, not mine.''

He folded his arms and rested one shoulder against the wall which was covered by a tiled mural suggesting a backdrop of rainforest and a waterfall. Tarzan at home in his jungle, she thought, taking in the damp strands of hair spilling across his forehead, and the gleam of muscles oiled with moisture from the sauna. His towel had slipped to hip level, and a fine scattering of dark chest hair arrowed down to meet it.

She licked suddenly dry lips and looked away, focusing on the waterfall over his shoulder. ''You deliberately let me think you were going to race me.''

''I didn't *say* I was going to. Never assume, Jac. Don't you teach that in self-defense classes?''

As a matter of fact she did. ''I don't usually make assumptions,'' she admitted.

''Then I must have distracted you. Good. That makes us even because you're very good at distracting me.'' He gave a teasing smile. ''Watching you from behind just now was highly distracting.''

He had set her up, but she couldn't find it in her heart to be mad at him. "Consider it part of your therapy."

He clutched at his heart, trying not very convincingly to look wounded. "Hardly therapeutic. That sassy walk of yours is enough to give a man palpitations."

She felt a few of her own, thinking of him observing her so blatantly. "Next time, walk in front of me then."

He looked smugly satisfied. "If I had, I'd have missed it."

She tried to appear disinterested but her heart was pounding. "Missed what?"

"You really shouldn't take such long strides wearing nothing but a towel, Jac. Or should I say, Madame Butterfly."

Horrified that she had revealed far more than she'd intended, she swatted at him blindly. "Next time, you sauna by yourself."

"What if an intruder should burst in and I should need defending?"

He looked more than capable of defending himself, but his comment snapped her back to painful reality. "I'll stand guard outside the door."

"Dressed like that? Now I really need a cold shower."

That made two of them, she thought. She was about to whirl around and head for the women's showers when she remembered. With a mocking courtly gesture, she stood to one side. "After you, Baron."

Chapter Eight

A day later the butterfly still haunted Mathiaz's thoughts as he waited in his office for Dr. Pascale's arrival. If their relationship was as impersonal as Jacinta kept telling him, how had Mathiaz known about her butterfly tattoo, and exactly where on her anatomy to look for it?

He started at finding Alain Pascale standing in front of his desk. "When did you sneak in?"

The doctor plunked his medical bag down on Mathiaz's desk, opened it and rummaged inside. "I never sneak. I knocked, but you were so preoccupied, you wouldn't have heard me if I'd shot in here out of a canon."

Mathiaz smiled at the doctor's characteristically colorful prose. "I told Lyons to let me know when you arrived."

"He isn't at his post. Where's your lovely minder today?"

"Jacinta's checking on things back at her academy.

Since I'm not going anywhere thanks to you, I told her that the RPD can take care of me while she takes a few hours off."

Pascale brushed this aside with one hand. "The Royal Protection Detail wasn't much use against your intruder the other night."

"Jacinta thinks the intruder has inside connections to have gotten past security so easily. The police are checking out the possibility."

Pascale nodded. "Smart lady, your Jacinta. Gutsy, too. I'm surprised some man hasn't swept her off her feet before now."

The prospect made Mathiaz more uncomfortable than he wanted the doctor to see. He said gruffly, "Maybe she doesn't want to be swept."

"I've yet to meet the woman who doesn't want to be swept. My Helen started out like Jacinta, clever, independent, career minded. Didn't matter one whit once love got into the picture."

According to Jacinta, love hadn't even shown itself as a blip on the horizon, far less entered the picture, Mathiaz thought gloomily. "Forget it, Alain, she's not interested," he said, hoping the doctor would take the hint and drop the subject.

Mathiaz should have known better. "Then it's up to you to get her interested."

"You're assuming I want to."

"If you didn't want to, you wouldn't be so fixated on her. Roll up your sleeve."

Mathiaz complied, and the doctor checked his blood pressure. "Disgustingly healthy," the doctor muttered. Mathiaz had already seen for himself that the reading was perfect.

Pascale put the equipment away and turned his attention to Mathiaz's injured leg. "Coming along just fine, in spite of your efforts to undo my handiwork," he said after his examination. "Next time, let the security people tackle the intruders, will you?"

Mathiaz ignored the comment, knowing that if Jacinta were in danger, he would do the same thing again, no matter what the cost to himself. "Would you do me a favor and tell Josquin I'm fine, so I can get back to work?" he asked. The Crown Regent had joked that he would allow the baron back into his office this morning on condition that he didn't spend more than a couple of hours working.

The doctor set his jaw. "Your leg may be recovered, but you're not fine as long as you're still missing a year's worth of memories."

"You said yourself I may never get them back." He let his tone ask how long he was supposed to put his life on hold.

"Have you seen the counselor I recommended, to help you deal with the possibility?" Pascale read the answer in Mathiaz's expression. "I thought not. You're as stubbornly self sufficient as every de Marigny I've ever known."

"As it happens, I have regained some memories," Mathiaz went on, knowing this would get the doctor's attention.

He was right. "How much have you remembered?"

"Prince Henry's funeral," Mathiaz supplied. "A few other fragments." He decided that Jacinta's butterfly was none of the doctor's business.

Pascale repacked his bag. "It's progress. Doesn't mean you're fully recovered yet."

The doctor's bedside manner definitely needed work, Mathiaz thought, not for the first time. Just as well he was an outstanding physician. Another idea occurred to him. "Alain, were you in Valmont when Jacinta worked for me the last time?"

The doctor's expression became wary. "I visited the château occasionally."

"Can you tell me what went on between us?"

"Shouldn't you ask her that?"

"I have done." His sigh telegraphed how far he'd gotten.

The doctor settled into a chair opposite the baron, and folded his arms. "What do you think went on?"

Mathiaz paused. "A lot more than she wants me to remember."

"Why would she keep such a thing from you?"

"I've asked myself the same question. The only answer making sense is that whatever was between us ended badly."

"You don't believe that?"

Mathiaz slammed his fist down on the desk. "I believe something went wrong, but what I feel whenever I'm with her is too strong to be—" what had Jacinta called it? "—wishful thinking on my part."

The doctor took a deep breath. "I don't know the whole story. I doubt anybody does except the two of you. But if it helps, I saw you with her a few times during that period, and I needed sunglasses to handle the glow radiating off the pair of you."

"Then we *were* involved?"

"If you weren't, Hollywood should send you a couple of Oscars for acting ability."

Mathiaz frowned. "According to Jacinta, the couple thing was our cover story."

Pascale got to his feet and reached for his bag. "Those Oscars are on the way."

"You think she really cared for me?"

Pascale closed his bag with a snap. "I'm not a relationship counselor. You'll have to look inside yourself to answer that one."

Mathiaz laced his tone with sarcasm. "Thanks for your help, Doctor."

The sarcasm washed off Pascale. "Anytime. I'll tell Prince Josquin you're fit to resume your normal duties, but you really should make time to see the counselor."

Mathiaz grinned hollowly. "I'll give the advice all the consideration it deserves."

Jacinta was glad to be back in her own world for a few hours. Or so she told herself, not sure how truthfully. The idea of offering her assistant, Shelley Hackett, a full partnership was growing in appeal.

Shelley had done a good job of running the academy in Jacinta's absence. The paperwork was in order, better than it would have been had Jacinta stayed in charge, she knew. Class numbers were up. She had no real reason to sit here, except a reluctance to return to the château and face Mathiaz again.

When he had remembered the butterfly tattoo, she had felt something freeze inside her, as she waited to see what else he would recall. So far nothing else had surfaced, but she could see that he was starting to question her denial of a relationship between them.

"Is everything to your liking, boss?" Shelley asked, poking her head around Jacinta's office door.

With a father in the American military, and a mother from Carramer, Shelley had inherited the loveliest combination of genes Jacinta could imagine. She was charming as well, not to mention a crack shot and a martial arts expert who regularly gave Jacinta a run for her money.

Jacinta grinned at her assistant and friend. "You know it is. You might have left me a small crisis to deal with."

Shelley smiled. "Duly noted. I'll arrange one for next time you stop by." She came into the office and perched on the edge of Jacinta's desk. "How are things at the palace?"

"Château," Jacinta corrected automatically. "We had a break-in a couple of days ago. The intruder got away by boat."

Shelley nodded. "I read about it in the papers. When you arrived this morning, I couldn't help noticing the nice set of bruises he left you with."

Jacinta touched her neck where the bruises were fading. "Not much of an advertisement for the academy."

"On the contrary. Registrations doubled next day, after folk read about the heroic way you tackled the intruder."

"Not so heroic. Lord Montravel had to stop the intruder from choking the life out of me."

Shelley sighed. "What a man. I gather he hasn't...you know."

Jacinta pretended ignorance. "No, I don't know."

"Remembered proposing to you."

"He didn't propose to me." The very thought made Jacinta's heart pound.

Shelley's eyes gleamed. "He would have done, if you'd stayed around long enough."

Her friend was one of the few people who knew about Jacinta's feelings for Mathiaz, and the phobia that stopped her from giving in to them. "But he didn't, and he isn't likely to now," she said.

"You don't think of his amnesia as a second chance? I know how much you cared about him."

Jacinta shook her head. "As far as the baron remembers, I'm there to do a job, that's all."

With a look of sympathetic understanding, Shelley levered herself off the desk. "I'd better go. I'm taking a class in five minutes. Sometimes I wish there were two of me, then I could be in here and out there at the same time."

"I know what you mean, but we'll catch up over coffee soon."

Shelley moved to the door, then said over her shoulder, "Think about what I said about second chances. It's more than most of us get."

Second chances. The words hung in the air after Shelley closed the door between them. Jacinta didn't believe in second chances, any more than she believed in destiny. There had been no second chance for Colin. Very nearly none for Mathiaz, after he sprang to her aid.

She thought of a training video for bodyguards she'd studied before going to work for Mathiaz. The tape had stressed that the first rule was to keep your client out of harm's way. Involving Mathiaz in a violent altercation meant she hadn't been doing her job. Calling palace security the moment she became aware of the intruder, would have been more effective than leaping to the rescue.

Furious at herself, she went cold at the thought of what could have happened to Mathiaz as a result of her recklessness. She owed it to both of them to resign before this went any further.

If he would let her.

The thought that he would probably refuse to accept her resignation frustrated her so much that she had shredded a piece of letterhead into small pieces before she realized what she was doing.

Giving vent to a sigh, she tossed the remnants of the letterhead away, and stalked to the window. The academy overlooked a park that was popular with families. In the late afternoon sun, small children played on the lush green grass while their parents looked on.

Children were another challenge. If her phobia wouldn't let her love one man, how would she cope with having a child depend on her totally? They were so small, so vulnerable. Protecting your own child was a human drive as old as time. Yet logic told her she couldn't protect them from everything. Sooner or later, life had to be experienced in all its diversity...and danger.

Fear flickered through her. Her need to wrap those she loved in cotton wool made motherhood seem even less possible for her than marriage.

Lost in her thoughts, she still heard the tiny creak her office door made as it eased open. Reflected in the window she saw a man come in. She spun around, her senses on full alert.

Her training made an assessment automatic. He was a little over two meters tall, clean shaven and well built. An open-necked white shirt was tucked into slim fitting charcoal jeans. He wore his dark hair on to his collar under a baseball cap. She couldn't see his eyes behind opaque Ray-Bans.

"Can I help you?" she asked, steadying her voice with an effort. There was a chance that he was a prospective student, although instinct made her doubt it.

"I'm looking for Jacinta Newnham."

The gruff voice was immediately familiar. "Mathiaz?" she said on a flash of suspicion.

He swept the baseball cap off his head, the long hair going with it. "Sprung. You must admit you didn't recognize me at first."

Fear for his safety argued with pleasure at seeing him. "What are you doing here?"

"Testing a theory." He removed the glasses and placed them and the cap on her desk. "I found the outfit in a closet at my office, and guessed I must have used it to go out incognito."

"How did you manage to leave the château without alerting security?"

"I attached myself to a tour group being shown around the public galleries. When they left, I left and hailed a cab to get here. Simple."

"Dangerous." She grabbed the hat by the hair and shook it at him. "You could get yourself killed pulling this stunt."

"Then I have pulled it before?"

She debated whether to answer. He had worked most of it out for himself. "You used it when you wanted to be alone with…a woman." She was horrified at how close she came to saying, "with me."

She felt annoyed with herself for not seeing through the disguise right away. Or recalling the last time he'd used it.

He had wanted them to go out on an ordinary date, impossible given the threat of the stalker. Overriding her concern, he'd persuaded her to buy the disguise then used it to slip out of the château on the heels of a tourist group, just as he'd done today.

Since she hadn't been able to convince him to remain safely within the compound, she'd waited for him in her car outside the walls. They had spent the day playing tourist in Perla.

Passing the Aimee Fountain still reminded her of how he'd playfully splashed her with water from it. The fountain dated back to 1892 and was adorned by a beautiful woman pouring water from a pitcher. Mathiaz had said the woman reminded him of Jacinta, although she doubted that she possessed such classic beauty.

"Who?" he demanded, startling her out of her reverie.

She struggled with a frown. "Excuse me?"

"The name of the woman I wanted to be alone with?"

Why did she have to be specific, knowing he would ask the obvious question. "How should I know? A gentleman doesn't discuss his love life."

His eyes shone with interest. "Unless it's with the lady in question."

She tossed her head, the short locks creating a less than satisfying effect. "Then you'll have to ask her, won't you."

"I believe I just did."

"You don't know for sure."

"Obviously not."

His bitter tone shook her. She felt cruel, although she hadn't intended to torment him about his memory loss. "Very well, you disguised yourself so we could meet," she admitted.

"For what reason?"

"Sightseeing."

His eyebrows lifted in obvious disbelief. "I sneaked out of the château in disguise to go sightseeing?"

She let her chin firm. Why hadn't she thought of sticking to the literal truth before? Mathiaz might read more into her explanation than she wanted him to, but without any memory of the events, he had no choice but to accept hers.

"With the increased security at the château, you said you felt stir-crazy and wanted to experience the city as an ordinary visitor. We went to all the usual haunts, the museum, the Heritage Center, the Aimee fountain."

His mouth turned down. "Sounds like we had a thrilling time."

"It was—educational." Especially when they held hands and kissed in the spray from the fountain. According to Carramer legend, lovers who kissed within reach of the spray were supposed to be bound together for all time.

Legend, not fact. And not remotely accurate in their case.

He retrieved the hat and settled it on his head, arranging the hair around his shoulders. "We'll start with the Center."

"You want to go there now?"

He replaced the hat and popped the Ray-Bans on his nose, the transformation so complete that she felt unnerved, although she knew that the simplest disguises were usually the most effective.

"Why not? Retracing our steps might help trigger some lost memories."

The last thing she wanted. She gestured toward her desk. "I still have work to do." There must be *something* Shelley had left undone.

"I'll go alone."

He knew perfectly well she wouldn't let him while his life was still under threat. Frustration settled around her like a cloak as she reached for her bag and sunglasses, and retrieved her gun from the safe. "We'll take my car."

The Heritage Center was Perla's newest and most adventurous architectural project. Dedicated to the monarch who had united the islands of Carramer into one nation centuries before, the center testified to the cultural richness of the kingdom.

To reach the center they had to pass the Royal Treasury, scene of the explosion that had robbed Mathiaz of his memory of the past year. She saw him studying the building. The damage to the heavily carved doors had been repaired, although part of the forecourt was still roped off and workmen were replacing the sandstone paving.

"Remember anything?" she asked.

His brow creased. "I wish I could. Seeing the place gives me a sense of unease, but nothing more. The explosion might never have happened."

She felt her mouth tighten into a grim line. "It happened."

He rubbed his calf, his expression rueful. "And left a painful souvenir."

Not the only one, she thought. "Does your leg still hurt?"

"Only with overuse. Normal walking feels fine, so there's no need to go easy on me this afternoon."

She let her eyebrow lift. "I wouldn't dream of it."

Situated on a peninsula within walking distance of the business district, the Heritage Center, actually three linked buildings each designed in the shape of one of Carramer's main islands, reflecting the kingdom's harmony with nature and the encircling ocean.

Each building showcased a different aspect of the kingdom's heritage. One was dedicated to the Mayats, the earliest known inhabitants of Carramer, who had reached the islands by sea two thousand years before.

The other two buildings were dedicated to the oceanic cultures comprising modern-day Carramer. There was also a performing arts arena, library, media rooms and classrooms.

Around the buildings wove a network of coral paths, where trees and plants important to the kingdom had been planted, interspersed with sites representing mythical events and times.

"I should do this more often," Mathiaz commented as they meandered along the path, reading the plaques explaining the significance of each site.

Edginess gripped her. Habit, she told herself. She needed to stay alert in case someone saw through Mathiaz's disguise. Or he remembered something she didn't want him to remember. So far no one had given them a second glance. Which left the memories as the main source of her unease.

She took a steadying breath. "What's stopping you?"

"Being royal has its downside," he pointed out.

"You mean, having to take a minder or at least a chauffeur with you everywhere?" The drivers were all trained members of the Royal Protection Detail, and doubled as bodyguards when needed, she knew.

He nodded. "Hardly a recipe for intimacy."

As if to demonstrate that today was different, he slid his hand into hers. The gesture was casual enough but her pulse picked up speed anyway, and she felt herself flush a little.

Moving away would be far too revealing, so she left her hand in his, struggling to subdue the excitement racing through her. Not panic, she noticed in some surprise. At least not yet.

They walked on and he began to enlarge on the stories on the plaques, impressing her with his knowledge of his country's history. "Bit of a hobbyhorse of mine," he confessed when she commented.

"They should make you patron of this place."

He gave a self-deprecating smile. "They already did."

"No wonder you can't drop in without causing a stir."

He was causing one now, but within her. As they walked, she had drifted closer until her body was aligned with his. The roaring sound of the blood in her ears drowned out his history lesson until all she could hear was the siren song of his nearness.

He heard it, too, because he stopped lecturing and pulled her off the path into the shelter of a banyan tree. It was late and they had the area to themselves. She almost wished they hadn't. If someone would only come along, she might be able to start breathing again.

No one came.

Mathiaz pushed his cap back and bent his head to Jacinta's. He was probably taking unfair advantage, but he couldn't stop himself. He had wanted to kiss her all afternoon. Giving her a history lesson had been the verbal equivalent of a cold shower, and was about as much use in defusing the firestorm of needs she made him feel. She was caring, funny and smart, all qualities he could love. It was frustrating not to know if he was falling in love again, or remembering something they'd shared before.

He skimmed his hand along the peaches-and-cream softness of her cheek and down her neck, feeling her pulse beat like a trapped bird against his fingers. Fear or anticipation? How could he tell her she had no need to fear him when he remembered nothing of what they had shared?

She had assured him he had never tried to force her into anything. He knew he wasn't forcing her now. Her mouth shaped to his so readily that he didn't doubt she wanted him as much as he wanted her.

So why wasn't she telling him everything she knew? He felt the ambivalence in her response, as if she was torn between wanting to kiss him and wanting to run away.

He lifted his head. "If I hurt you, Jacinta, I'm more sorry than you'll ever know."

Confusion clouded her lovely eyes. "What makes you think you hurt me?"

"I must have said or done something you don't want to talk about."

As she opened her mouth to protest, he pressed a finger over her lips, silencing her. "It doesn't matter, because I won't hurt you this time, I promise."

"This time?" He heard the shiver in her voice.

"Those memories may be gone for good. Perhaps it's for the best, because we can start over again from now."

"You're asking a great deal."

"More than I know. I understand. One day you'll tell me what happened, and I'll make things right if I can. All right?"

She met his gaze falteringly, but didn't look away. After a moment she nodded.

Sweet relief coursed through him. The fear he saw in her eyes was mirrored in his own dread that she would deny them this chance. "I'm glad, because I'm falling in love with you. So much about you calls to me—not only your beauty, but your strength and tenderness, and your wonderful sense of humor. I can't believe this is happening for the first time. It feels too right."

Jacinta felt alarm flare through her. Surrounded by history, she wondered how much could actually be changed. Not this, evidently. Everything she had done to change the course of her relationship with Mathiaz had still led them to the same point.

"Oh, Mathiaz, it isn't that simple."

"It's as simple as we want it to be. Unless you want to tell me why it has to be complicated."

Panic clawed at her, strangling her, urging her to run, to hide, anything but stand and listen to him tell her all over again that he loved her. Only duty held her to the spot. She had to think of his safety. While he remained under threat, running away was a luxury she couldn't allow herself.

She stayed.

"You don't have to feel the same way yet," he went on, misreading her silence. "For now, I want you to know how I feel about you, but I won't say any more until you're ready. Okay?"

Grateful for the reprieve, she said, "Okay."

"Good. Let's continue the history lesson."

If he was aware of her inattention, he didn't comment. As if to compensate, she found herself focusing on small details, from how his fingers curled around hers, to the thoughtful way he moderated his long strides to save her working so hard to keep up.

She also kept an eye on the activities going on around them, alert to any possible threat to Mathiaz. Far from impeding her alertness, his declaration of love had sharpened her senses to a degree she found thoroughly disturbing.

As she found *him* thoroughly disturbing.

Mathiaz hadn't asked for her love, but she knew he wanted it. He didn't know that she was incapable of giving him what he wanted. Accepting his love would trigger her phobia until she was driven to leave, just like last time.

The pain of the realization was so intense that if she hadn't been keeping a careful watch, she would have almost missed seeing the man. He seemed to be looking right at her, then he hurried away. Awareness came a split second later. "That's Andre Zenio."

Her muttered comment brought Mathiaz's head around. "Where?"

Too late. She pointed ahead of them. "He disappeared in the direction of the Treasury building." She looked at Mathiaz. His disguise was still in place. "What is Zenio doing here, now?"

"Not following me, at least not looking like this."

She envied Mathiaz his certainty. Her heart was pounding at the nearness of a threat to him.

Mathiaz frowned. "This is a public place. He has a right to be here."

"To be on the safe side, we'll take the other path back to the car," she said.

She kept her eyes open but saw no more of Zenio, although her heart rate didn't slow until they were on their way back to the château with no sign of anyone following them. On the way, Mathiaz removed his disguise so they wouldn't be stopped at the château gates.

If her hands weren't clamped around the steering wheel, she knew they'd be shaking. She was furious with herself for giving so much of her attention to Mathiaz until they were almost on top of Zenio.

She was tempted to tell the baron there and then that a love-struck bodyguard was no good to him. But the admission would reveal how much she cared for him, and she was fairly sure how he would react. He'd assure her he understood, and promise to help her overcome her phobia. He would end up protecting her, instead of the other way around.

She kept her thoughts to herself.

Chapter Nine

Unable to contain her energy, Jacinta paced up and down Mathiaz's office. He didn't really mind. In short shorts the color of clotted cream, she moved with the grace of a young deer.

Her filmy floral top looked as if it was made from a scarf wound around her neck, hiding the fading bruises from her brush with the intruder. The scarf crossed in front over her breasts before being tied in back. As she paced, she revealed tantalizing sections of golden skin where the scarf pulled away from the shorts at her waist.

Mathiaz wondered idly if a tug on the knotted end would unravel the scarf, then chased the thought from his mind. In Jacinta's present mood, she was more likely to bite his head off than to welcome his touch.

"I don't understand. The man I saw at the Heritage Center *was* Zenio," she insisted.

Mathiaz laced his fingers together on the desk top and looked down at them, trying to concentrate, which he found hard to do while watching her. "Palace security has kept tabs on him since you thought you recognized him during the break-in. According to them, during the time we were at the Heritage Center yesterday, he was taking his wife and new baby to the hospital for a checkup."

Anger flared through her. "Since I *thought* I recognized him?"

He looked up. "I'm sure you believe you saw him both times, Jac."

"Evidently you don't."

He didn't like being the target of her anger. "My opinion doesn't matter. He had a watertight alibi."

"Alibis can be faked."

"Not with the staff at the hospital as witnesses to his whereabouts the first time, and the security detail the second." The baron let his voice crackle with annoyance. "This has gone on long enough. Andre Zenio stalked me once, but he was caught and paid the price. He earned his parole. The man is entitled to get on with his life without being under constant suspicion."

She placed her hands flat on his desk, the pose straining the scarf wrap to the limit and making him drag in a choked breath. "Someone planted that bomb at the Treasury."

A hint of orchid perfume wafted over him, making him want to wrap his arms around her and kiss away her annoyance. He reined in the impulse. "Obviously. That's why the police and our own security people are working to find the culprit. Obsessing about Andre Zenio isn't going to help."

Her eyes slitted. "So you think I'm obsessing, do you?"

This conversation wasn't going the way he'd planned it. When he awoke this morning, Mathiaz had intended to invite Jacinta to be his guest at tonight's fireworks display to lead off tomorrow's Journey Day holiday, the Carramer festival commemorating the unification of the islands into one kingdom.

Mathiaz's cousin, Josquin and his family, and Mathiaz's brother, Eduard, home on leave from the navy, would be in the party. Mathiaz had had some thought of getting his family used to the idea that Jacinta was becoming more to him than a bodyguard, if they hadn't already guessed. Having her join the royal family while she was off duty would start tongues wagging, exactly the way he wanted them to.

Not that Mathiaz intended them to spend too long with the royal family. After he had done his duty at the festival, he had intended to bring Jacinta back to his villa for a private celebration of the holiday.

He still owed her a private movie screening, and the prospect of spending an evening in the dark with her had a lot of appeal, although he doubted how much of the film they would manage to see.

''Perhaps obsessing is too strong a word,'' he tried.

''You bet it is.''

''You have to admit, you're seeing this man everywhere.''

''Only everywhere you happen to be.'' She straightened. ''Don't you find that an odd coincidence.''

Mathiaz though for a moment. ''You're forgetting another obvious possibility.''

He saw her eyes narrow. ''What?''

''You were with me on both occasions.''

A flash of interest lit her eyes. ''You think I could be his target this time?''

He shook his head. ''Not Zenio, but whoever you saw.''

The interest faded, replaced by annoyance. "I am a martial arts expert. Making split-second judgments is part of that."

"Split-second judgments aren't always the right ones," he reminded her quietly. "In the dark in the heat of a fight, and yesterday when you were focused on me, you weren't exactly in the best position to see things clearly."

He knew he was projecting his own feelings onto her. His judgment had definitely been clouded yesterday. Slipping out of the château unguarded, even in disguise, hadn't been smart, but his need to be alone with her had outweighed everything.

Since injuring his leg, he'd had a treadmill brought to his office so he could fit in extra exercise between meetings. Jacinta walked to the machine and fiddled with the settings, keeping her back to him. "What makes you think I was distracted yesterday?"

What a beautiful back, he thought, even set as stiffly as it was now. The knotted scarf covered little, and he felt the urge to run his hand over her smooth skin. He could almost feel the shudder he would elicit. His voice felt strained as he said, "I know I was."

So was she, Jacinta thought, playing with the computer on the treadmill.

She tapped in a setting and stepped on to the machine. The motor whirred softly as the treadmill started rolling under her feet, urging her into a steady walk. The movement helped to discharge some of her tension. No matter how many alibis Zenio produced, she knew what she had seen.

It hurt that Mathiaz didn't believe her. She shot him a glance, noting the stubborn set of his jaw. He thought she was obsessed with one man to the exclusion of other possibilities. Was she? She tapped the computer, picking up the pace.

She was afraid for the baron. She hadn't forgotten the live bullet Zenio had sent to Mathiaz just before the police picked him up the last time. Would the next one be found in the barrel of a gun? A fist tightened around her heart. She had to trust her instincts on this. Zenio was somehow involved and must be stopped before he could harm Mathiaz.

But could she trust her judgment when she was so caught up with the baron that her own feelings scared her? Her friend Shelley had called his amnesia a second chance. What good was a second chance if everything worked out exactly as it had the first time?

Mathiaz felt his throat go dry as he watched Jacinta on the treadmill. Legs as long as hers should be illegal, especially when moving gracefully at a fast walk that reminded him of a thoroughbred in action.

He wanted to haul her off the treadmill and into his arms where he could kiss some sense into her. He had no doubt that she believed she had seen Zenio on both occasions, although she couldn't have done.

"What would Zenio have been doing near the Treasury anyway?" he said, thinking out loud.

She looked at him thoughtfully without slackening her pace. He switched his gaze to her face but that only made him remember what a kissable mouth she had. He was halfway out of his chair before he stopped himself. Instinct told him if he wanted to get anywhere with her, he had to proceed with care.

He hadn't missed the panic in her eyes yesterday when he told her he was falling in love with her. For some reason, that scared her. He knew it wasn't because she didn't feel anything for him. When they kissed, she had been as lost in passion as he had. He had felt the earthquake tremors of her response, and the hunger of her lips shaping to his. So there had to be more to her fear.

Instinctively he knew that his missing memories held the key. Why couldn't he remember? He pushed his hair back from his face with both hands, massaging his temples with his fingertips to dull a sudden hammering of pain.

She stopped the treadmill and moved to his side. "Headache?"

"Colossal one."

She turned away. "Are you taking the painkillers Dr. Pascale prescribed for you?"

He caught her wrist. "I don't need pills, Jac. I need answers."

There it was again, that quick flare of panic in her gaze, spearing him to his gut. He hated being the cause of her fear, although he knew somehow he was.

"I can't give you answers, Mathiaz," she said unsteadily.

He resisted the urge to shake her, already feeling brutal enough. "You can't or you won't?"

"Both."

The simple statement stopped him in his tracks. He stood up and pushed her captive hand behind her, pulling her against him. Sheer wanton desire tore through him. He hooked his free hand around her shoulders, sliding his palm along her neck until her head tilted back. Her mouth was half open in protest and he shamelessly took advantage of it to kiss her as he'd needed to do all morning.

The kiss satisfied one need but aroused others, until he felt lightning bolts of desire shooting through him.

He wouldn't have been surprised to see actual sparks flying off him, so powerful was the response she aroused in him.

He had never been shy around women, believing that sexuality was a gift to be cherished and celebrated. But he felt unaccountably shy now, reluctant to take advantage of her when she was obviously terrified of what he made her feel.

"You know I care about you," he said against her mouth. The taste of her was so wonderful that he wanted to taste more and more, but he used all his willpower to keep a whisper of distance between them.

Her tongue darting out to moisten her lips was almost his undoing. "I know."

"For some reason, that frightens you. Why?"

Her lashes veiled her gaze from him. "What makes you think I'm frightened?"

"Your body is as rigid as a board, and when I look into your eyes, I see fear."

She gave a small shake of her head. "Not of you."

"Then what?"

For a moment, he thought she was going to tell him at last, then she looked away.

He masked his disappointment and released her. In his teens, a wise old horse trainer from Nuee, Carramer's smallest inhabited island, had shown Mathiaz how to tame the island's wild horses through gentleness and empathy, instead of using brute force and fear. The man's skill had seemed miraculous to Mathiaz, as he watched him gentle a wild stallion. At the first approach, the magnificent creature had quivered with fear. By the time the man finished, the stallion was nuzzling his hand and following him around the arena.

Where he and Jacinta were concerned, there was

plenty of time, as the wise man had assured him over and over. ''Nature can't be remade in a hurry,'' he'd told Mathiaz. ''Time is the great healer, the key to changing fear into love.''

Mathiaz resolved to give Jac whatever time she needed, although he had a fair idea of the cost to himself. He could already feel the strain of holding back, when everything in him wanted to take her now, without ceremony, to ravish her until they were both beyond reason, satisfying the oldest drives known to man.

He made himself step away from her before he allowed himself to forget the old horse breaker's advice.

Jacinta hadn't missed the flare of primitive need in his gaze. She felt it within herself, too, and almost wished he hadn't been so strong. What would she have done if he'd simply pushed through her resistance, and taken her here and now?

A thrill of exhilaration soared through her, before it was damped by the throb of her pulse. A lump climbed into her throat. Not fair, she thought. To want something so much, yet be held back by senseless fear from reaching out and grasping the prize. She almost sobbed her frustration, turning away from Mathiaz to hide her shame.

He wouldn't allow her to retreat. He pulled her against him, the gesture friendly this time, without the passion that would have triggered alarm bells inside her. ''Come here, Jac. You have nothing to fear from me.''

Shuddering, she buried her face against his shoulder, feeling his warmth and strength flood through her, restoring her. She was reluctant to acknowledge the tiny flame of hope that flickered inside her at his touch. Could he really be content with the little she was able to give him?

He needed a woman who would give herself to him without reservation, matching him with the intensity of her desire. As long as Jacinta let herself be limited by fear, she couldn't be that woman.

She almost laughed. How could she be so fearless in other ways, throwing herself into unarmed combat, and excelling on the firing range, yet be such a coward in love?

He felt the shake of her shoulders she tried to repress, and lifted her chin so she met his gaze. "What's so amusing?"

"Nothing in particular." She could hardly tell him the truth.

He released her. "Someday I hope you'll let me in on the joke." As well as her other secrets.

She made her tone light. "You never know your luck."

Letting her go, he rested one thigh on the edge of his desk, and she moved to the window, putting some much needed distance between them. Below her, workmen scurried about the grounds, carrying building materials. "What's going on down there?"

"They're setting up a temporary viewing platform for tonight's fireworks."

Over her shoulder she shot him a concerned look. "In the grounds of the château? Aren't they being held in Perla?" They had been every year since she came to Carramer.

"This year Josquin decided to stage a special festival at Château Valmont in honor of the ascension of Crown Prince Christophe to the Valmont throne."

Jacinta remembered seeing the news of how the tiny heir had been found living in America. His mother, Princess Sarina, had been adopted by an American family without learning of her royal heritage until she was an adult. Prince Josquin, the one to find her, had fallen headlong in love with her, their marriage providing a fairy-tale ending to the saga.

Jacinta felt a frown of worry settle over her eyes. "Couldn't the Crown Regent find a safer way to celebrate finding the Valmont heir?" Opening the château to the public with a mad bomber on the loose struck her as foolhardy to say the least.

Mathiaz gave her a look of agreeing with her, but for different reasons. He didn't like the idea of sharing her with a crowd. "Josquin doesn't believe in giving in to threats. As far as he's concerned, tonight is business as usual. A controlled number of visitors will be allowed into the grounds which will be crawling with police, as well as a full complement of RPD. All the royal residences will be guarded against unauthorized entry."

He shifted his position, toying with a gold pen he and a visiting dignitary had used to sign an important trade agreement. "I want you to accompany me to the festivities tonight."

She swung around. "Of course I'll be there."

"I don't mean as my bodyguard. I want you to be my date."

He saw her digest this. "You want us to use our old cover story in public?"

"Not a cover story, the real thing."

"Mathiaz, I don't think so."

The tremor in her voice baffled him. She had been more than willing to accompany him in her official capacity, even to pretend to be involved with him. Why was there a problem because he wanted the role to be real?

He decided to bite the bullet and ask her.

She prowled around his office as if it was barely large enough to contain her restlessness. "A few minutes ago, I got the impression that you were willing to wait for an explanation until I was ready. You waited what? All of five minutes."

Her halfhearted attempt at humor didn't fool him. "So I'm impatient. Are you surprised?"

She picked up a ship in a bottle, another diplomatic souvenir, and gave the ornament all her attention, although she must have seen it dozens of times before. Abruptly she put it down and faced him. "Not really. Impatience is one of your qualities."

He made a face. "Not one of my better ones."

"Probably not. You do have other redeeming features."

He decided against asking what she thought they were. They were unlikely to be the qualities he wanted her to see in him. When had her good opinion become so important? Along with so much more that he wanted to know, the moment was lost in the fog of his memory. "I still want you with me," he said.

"I'll be glad to attend the festivities as your bodyguard," she insisted.

"I don't want the woman at my side to be armed to the teeth, with eyes for everyone in the crowd but me."

She shrugged, but her gaze was clouded. "That's what I'm here for."

"Not tonight. Tonight I want you wearing your prettiest finery, with your hair fluffed out the way you wear it when you're off duty."

She touched the strands self-consciously. "I didn't think you'd noticed."

"I don't remember when I did, but in my mind I can picture you in a long black gown, with glittery stuff in your hair that made it sparkle like starlight. And don't tell me I'm imagining things,'' he said when she looked as if she was about to argue. ''I may not be able to remember when you came to me dressed like that, but I sure as blazes know you did.''

''I wouldn't dream of arguing with you, Baron,'' she said primly. ''If you command me to dress up and appear tonight as your date, I will of course, obey.''

''You know damned well I don't want you to accompany me because I command you to.''

She shook her head. ''Nothing less will get me there, other than in my official capacity.''

He gave a tired sigh. ''Then consider yourself commanded. But leave your blasted gun behind. For a change, I want to do the protecting.''

''I don't always have a gun on me.''

''That's fairly obvious.'' There was nowhere in the filmy top or skimpy shorts where she could conceal a firearm, however compact.

A flush sprang to her features as his gaze roved over her outfit. ''This morning it's in my purse.''

''At the fireworks this evening, I don't want you armed at all.''

''You mean this, don't you?''

Now she was getting the idea, Mathiaz thought. ''Tonight you can leave the heroics to the police and security detail, and relax.''

A smile played around her mouth. ''Is that an order, too?''

''If necessary.''

He would like to order her to enjoy herself, but knew some things couldn't be commanded. Her enjoyment would depend on his skill and attentiveness, a task he would undertake with pleasure.

He hadn't mentioned what they would do after the fireworks display ended. Time enough to suggest a stroll in the moonlight and an intimate supper after she had adjusted to the change in their relationship. Mathiaz remembered his teacher's advice, time was the key to changing fear into love.

He couldn't afford to let impatience get the better of him when he had so much at stake.

Chapter Ten

Jacinta knew exactly which outfit Mathiaz was remembering. In the sanctuary of her suite, she held it against her, looking in the mirror and remembering, too.

She had worn it the night he had told her he loved her. There had been no fireworks, except those going off inside her head. No shortage of those. She felt them now, building to an intensity she knew could lead only to one outcome.

She would stay as long as she could, allow him to kiss her and pledge his love to her, until fear gave her feet wings. Then she would pack and leave, just like last time—unless she could manage to overcome her phobia and make herself stay.

Her breath hitched. Could she do it?

From bitter experience, she knew what was involved. The fear that had made her run away from him the last time would be intense, stronger than anything she had to deal with in her present job. An intruder or a potential assassin she could fight. The threat coming from inside her was far harder to combat for being invisible and illogical.

The stakes were also higher.

If she could make herself stay, what could she and Mathiaz become to each other? At the very notion, her throat threatened to close but she took deep breaths until her heartbeat slowed. She could do this. She would do this.

Somehow she had to fight her way past the belief that something terrible would happen to Mathiaz if she allowed herself to love him. She had never felt so motivated to try.

Tempted to wear something different as a symbol of how she wanted things to change, she threw the garment on the bed with a sigh, knowing no other would do when Mathiaz came for her tonight. If she could get one of the servants to track down some glitter spray for her hair, she would be wearing that as well.

Her record at changing history was unimpressive anyway, so why not ride the wave of déjà vu and see where it took her? He had asked her to wear the dress he had dredged out of his unreliable memory.

If she appeared in anything else, she risked undermining his confidence in his recovered memories, maybe even slowing his progress back to full health. Besides, knowing Mathiaz, he would probably order her to change anyway. And what she wore wasn't going to help her to overcome her fear. She was the only one who could do that.

The garment wasn't actually a dress, although she could understand why Mathiaz remembered differently. At the hips, it divided into palazzo pants so softly flowing that they looked like a skirt until she moved.

The top half was a sleeveless shell with a high back

and a deep vee neckline that exposed the cleft between her breasts. Shrugging her robe off her shoulders, she peered into the mirror. The bruises around her neck were almost gone. She would conceal the last traces under a black velvet ribbon, so the low neckline wouldn't be a problem, except possibly for its effect on Mathiaz.

This time a frisson of excitement overlaid her instinctive rush of anxiety. She was pleased to recognize the blood pounding in her head as pure, naked desire, although she wasn't sure if such an alarming sensation was progress. Fear and desire were such close cousins, she would have to work hard to separate them when the time came.

For come it would. Tonight, if the passion she had seen in Mathiaz's gaze in his office this morning was any guide. He wanted her. He had wanted her for longer than he remembered, and she had wanted him for about the same length of time, only her phobia preventing her from acting on her desire. Tonight she was determined not to let fear come between them.

By eight that evening, she was as ready as she was likely to be.

Mathiaz was punctual as always. Her blood stirred at the picture he made in dark pants and a white jacket cut in military style, with epaulettes on the shoulders and a loop of gold braid across his chest. The uniform was traditional, related more to his royal position than any military rank. Not many men could wear such an outfit and look regal enough to take her breath away. Mathiaz managed it easily.

He wasn't unmoved, she saw as he stilled in her doorway. In the heartbeat of silence, his gaze paid homage to her appearance. Then he dragged in a deep breath. "You look wonderful," he said in a low voice.

Stepping closer, he brushed her cheek as if to assure himself that she was real. "I remember this dress." His brow wrinkled as he took his hand away. "But it isn't a dress, is it?"

She swirled around in front of him, enough to show off the divided skirt. "You really do remember, don't you?"

"Not as much as I wish I could."

She swallowed around a lump clogging her throat. "You could always use your imagination."

His dark gaze assured her he was already following her advice. "If I keep doing that, we'll never make it to the fireworks."

Would she care? Only the panic threatening to rise inside her told her she would. She fought the sensation. "I guess we'd better join the rest of your party."

"Josquin's party, not mine. As long as I appear at the official program to show publicly that I'm all right, I can do as I choose for the rest of the night."

The warmth in his voice told her exactly how he would prefer to spend the time. The tightness in her chest increased. She could do this, she reminded herself. She would never have more of an incentive. "How do you choose to spend it?"

He leveled a provocative look at her. "Do you need to ask?"

She shook her head. To please him she had styled her hair so the curls clustered around her face. And the staff had come through with the glitter spray. The ethereal result had startled even her when she looked in the mirror. She looked softer, more feminine. Not so much a bodyguard as a body in serious need of guarding.

"No," she admitted softly.

He touched one of the curls, twining the hair around his finger. "No isn't a word I hope to hear tonight."

She cleared her throat. "I meant no, I didn't need to ask."

"Good. We understand one another."

He wanted to make love to her tonight. He didn't have to spell it out. The strength of his desire communicated in the way he looked at her, touched her. She felt torn in two. Wanting him as she had never wanted another man. Fearing the power of her own desires.

She had never allowed herself to become so close to a man before. Fear had always driven her away. She felt it building now, as a pounding at her temples and a dampness in her palms, until she willed herself to calmness. How could she be so afraid of something she wanted so much?

"You'll need a wrap in case the night becomes cool," he said, breaking her anxious train of thought.

She picked up her wrap, so finely woven that it felt like gossamer in her hands.

He took it from her and regarded it dubiously. "This wisp of a thing won't keep you warm."

"You'd be surprised."

"It feels as light as spiderweb."

"You're supposed to be able to pass the whole thing through a wedding ring, although I haven't tried it," she said.

He let a slow smile develop. "Where's a wedding ring when you need one?"

Her fear edged higher, almost out of her control. She pressed her fingertips together hard, striving for calm. It didn't work. "Mathiaz, I..."

Before she could finish he said, "Whenever I'm with

you, I think of all kinds of things I've never wanted before, like wedding rings and happy-ever-afters."

She masked her tension with a smile. "How do you know you've never had those thoughts before?"

She hated being the cause of his frown. "You're right, I wouldn't know. I don't suppose you'd tell me if we'd discussed them during the last year?"

"We didn't," she said with absolute honesty. She hadn't allowed herself to stay with him long enough to get to that stage.

"I'm glad."

Disappointment jolted through her. Was he teasing her with his talk of happy-ever-after? "Mind telling me why?" she asked, hearing the brittle note in her voice.

He let a slow smile spread across his handsome features. "Because when we do, I want to remember every detail."

"Oh." Her sigh whispered between parted lips. "This memory loss is really hard for you, isn't it?"

His smile faded. "Sometimes. Maybe I should take Dr. Pascale's advice and see the counselor he recommended."

"Why haven't you?"

He started to pace, but checked himself. "Because it means accepting that those months are gone from my memory for good, and I refuse to believe that."

Unable to stop herself, she touched the back of her hand to his cheek. "You never were one for giving up."

He caught her hand and brought it to his lips. The gesture speared her with longing. "I don't intend to give up now. Every so often I have a glimmer of memory, like your dress. It gives me hope."

"Me, too." As soon as she spoke the words, she knew she meant them. She wanted him to get his memory back, although he wouldn't be pleased with her when he did. He would remember how hurt and confused he had been when she refused to explain why she had to leave. She didn't expect him to understand that she hadn't left because she didn't want to be with him, but because she wanted to so much that the very thought struck panic deep into her soul.

Outwardly no one could guess, least of all Mathiaz. She had spent years refining her ability to hide her phobia until there were times when she even thought of herself as fearless.

Certainly she had no compunction about throwing herself into a fight at the academy. Riding, shooting, defensive driving all came as easily to her as breathing. Yet put love in the picture and she became a quivering mess.

If she could be granted one miracle, she would wish for Mathiaz to regain only the memory of their love, without remembering how she had ended it. She didn't think she could bear his disappointment with her a second time.

He draped the wrap carefully around her shoulders. When his fingertips brushed her nape, she shivered. Feeling the tremor, he pressed his lips to the same spot and she suppressed a moan. "Do you know what I really want?" he murmured without lifting his head.

The brush of his mouth against her bare skin was sheer torment. She could imagine what he wanted because she wanted the same thing so badly she ached with it. "Oh Lord, yes," she agreed.

He lifted his head, revealing eyes cloudy with desire. Hers felt the same. "This could be the shortest royal appearance on record," he said, sounding strained.

"Must we go at all?" Perhaps if he took her now,

when her entire being vibrated with wanting him, everything would be all right.

She saw him square his shoulders and take a steadying breath. "Duty," he said. "Sometimes it's hell being royal."

She tried for a shaky smile around her disappointment. "Sometimes it's hell when you're not."

He offered her his arm. "Josquin and the others will be waiting for us."

She tucked her hand into his arm thinking how long it had been since she had permitted herself to feel this close to a man. Waiting for the expected rush of anxiety, she was surprised when all she felt was a rising sense of excitement.

The night was glorious. She was in the company of a wonderful man, not as his minder, but as the woman he wanted by his side. What could she possibly have to fear?

Her mood was buoyant as they crossed the springy grass to where the dais had been set up for the royal family to view the fireworks, and be seen by the visitors already thronging the gardens. Mathiaz had told her that on the other islands of Isle des Anges and Nuee, the rest of the royals were participating in similar activities, Journey Day being one of Carramer's most important holidays.

Not surprising, she thought. Peace and unity were achievements worth celebrating.

"Happy?" Mathiaz murmured close to her ear.

She nodded. "Of course." His expression told her he felt the same way.

Prince Josquin looked regally handsome with Princess Sarina by his side and their baby son, Prince Christophe between them. The little boy's eyes shone with excitement at the entertainment to come. Jacinta smiled at him, knowing how he felt. Shyly he smiled back.

Josquin and Sarina greeted her warmly, although Josquin's eyebrows tilted in evident surprise when he realized that Mathiaz has brought Jacinta to the festivities as his date. She was seated beside Princess Sarina, with Mathiaz on her right.

As she took her seat she surveyed the crowd from sheer force of habit. Mathiaz had said he didn't want her guarding him tonight, but that was no excuse for abandoning her responsibilities. He was still in danger and she'd never forgive herself if anything happened to him.

The thought made her heart pick up speed until she made an effort to breathe normally. Nothing was going to happen to him. They were surrounded by his family, the Valmont police and members of the Royal Protection Detail.

As she let her gaze skim over the crowd, she nodded to the RPD people she recognized and got nods of response from those in uniform. She knew better than to acknowledge the ones in civvies she spotted mingling with the visitors.

One face jumped out at her from the crowd. The baron's equerry, Barrett Lyons. He looked around furtively as he spoke to a man Jacinta could again swear was Andre Zenio.

But it couldn't be Zenio. According to the report she had seen from the RPD earlier in the day, the police had granted Zenio permission to travel to Nuee with his wife and new baby. He was spending the holiday with his parents, and was required to report to the Nuee police regularly while on the island.

When she looked again, the equerry was still there but there was no sign of the Zenio lookalike. Jacinta's flesh crawled. She wasn't going to let her feelings for Mathiaz cloud her judgment. She couldn't possibly have seen Zenio because he wasn't here. Still feeling uneasy, she dragged her attention back to the entertainment.

As they rose for the playing of the Carramer national anthem, "From Sea to Stars," she found herself studying the royal family, wondering if she would have the strength to commit herself to marriage and motherhood as her countrywoman, Sarah, had done so brilliantly.

As the music ended and she resumed her seat, Jacinta shook off the possibility. Too soon and too daunting. First she had to overcome her panic every time she considered a close relationship with Mathiaz. Only then could she think of the future. She was disturbed by how much she wanted to.

The program started, claiming her attention. First came a storyteller, a descendant of the Mayat people who had populated Carramer a millennium before. She told the story of the king whose ancient journey had united the islands into one peaceful kingdom. Jacinta had heard the legend before, but this telling of it moved her almost to tears, although she wasn't Carramer born.

Little Christophe's expression was rapt. He had been born in America, Jacinta knew, but the throne of Valmont was his birthright, and he looked so at home that she envied him. So young and already sure of his place in the world. With a sigh, she focused on the storyteller who ended her tale with the traditional words, "And so the Carramer of our hearts was born."

Applause erupted like gunfire. Instinctively Jacinta tensed, then felt Mathiaz's hand slip into hers. His grip, warm and firm, soothed her soul. As Crown Regent Josquin gave a stirring speech about the future of the province. Mathiaz rose and thanked the visitors for the many well wishes he had received during his recovery, and spoke about the links between Carramer's past and present.

A choir sang. The orchestra played. The current Carramer pop sensation took to the stage and soon had the crowd clapping along with the fast beat of her song, Jacinta included.

She should be blissfully happy, she thought. So why did she feel an edge of tension, as if something terrible was going to happen? She had scanned the crowd a dozen times but had seen no more of Zenio's clone.

Lack of control, she concluded as yet another performer took the stage. As Mathiaz's bodyguard, she could take action if anything untoward happened. Being on the sidelines bothered her.

She felt a frown start. Was her ego the problem? No, the problem was Mathiaz. She wasn't comfortable being excluded from his protection team at such a risky time, but most of her anxiety stemmed from the reason why he hadn't wanted her on duty tonight. He wanted to make love to her.

She'd been hiding from that simple, inescapable fact all through the celebration. Not because she didn't want him to make love to her. She wanted it more than she had ever wanted anything. But bitter experience warned her how easily her own doubts could keep her from her heart's desire.

Mathiaz nudged her gently. "Looks like the fireworks are about to start."

In her heart they had already started, she thought, keeping silent, not wanting to spoil his enjoyment of the evening.

The stage lights flickered to blackness, leaving only a dim glow around the orchestra, which struck up an emotional symphonic score. Suddenly a galaxy of strobing stars shot across the sky, earning gasps from the crowd.

Jacinta found herself grinning as broadly at little Prince Christophe when a giant, glittering comet streaked overhead, showering the watchers with stars and leaving a shimmering afterimage in the night sky.

She caught her breath as a dazzling, color-changing chrysanthemum blossomed overhead. Then the whole sky lit with a rain of fiery color. "This is amazing," she said, gripping Mathiaz's hand tighter.

He didn't seem to mind, his gaze settling on her in the vivid afterglow of the effect. "Amazing," he agreed for her ears alone.

From the warmth in his look, she knew he didn't mean the fireworks.

More chrysanthemums blossomed, their appearance timed perfectly to the orchestral score. Lances, waterfalls, fountains and more comets followed until the sky was streaked with red, yellow, green, blue, gold and silver. Each rush of light and color received cheers and applause, Jacinta cheering as loudly as anyone.

A huge rocket streaked skyward, trailing a luminescent, milky-white starfield. Reaching the zenith of its flight, it exploded directly above them, the sound deafening for a moment.

As the explosion died away, Jacinta felt Mathiaz's grip almost crush her hand. She looked at him in concern, her worry increasing as the afterglow illuminated his set expression.

"Did the explosion trigger a memory?"

He nodded, looking so grim that she wondered what the explosion had unleashed. He was also in pain, she gathered from the tension threading around his mouth and eyes.

He got to his feet with an obvious effort, shrugging off the hand she offered to assist him. "Let's get out of here."

The rocket had been the climax of the festivities, because the lights came back on and she saw the people around them standing, preparing to move. Mathiaz went to Prince Josquin and made their farewells. Josquin looked concerned but she saw Mathiaz shake his head, refusing whatever help his cousin had offered.

"What is it? What have you remembered?" she asked as they walked back across the grass to his villa. Behind them, music played and people were dancing on the lawns, in no hurry to go home, unlike Mathiaz.

"I'll tell you when we're inside."

Why wouldn't he tell her now? Oh lord, had he remembered how she had walked out on him the last time, throwing his declaration of love back in his face? She knew hers was ashen as she considered the possibility. What else would make him sound so angry with her?

Her spirits sank. She had known this moment would come, had even hoped for it in order for Mathiaz to regain his memory. But she wasn't ready to pay the price. She knew he wouldn't want to have anything more to do with her, and the thought almost broke her heart.

He said no more until they had passed through the security cordon and were safely back within the walls of his villa, in the salon where he had intended to show her the movie. No candles illuminated a romantic setting tonight. How different that evening had been from this one.

Barrett Lyons was there ahead of them. Coincidence or signaled by the baron? She didn't know and didn't care, but wished the equerry would leave them alone.

The man bothered her. She couldn't stand people who hovered.

At a terse request from the baron, Lyons went to the bar and poured a brandy, handing it to Mathiaz. When he offered her one, she shook her head, wanting only to get this over with. Lyons withdrew into the shadows, fussily rearranging the bar until she wanted to scream at him to go away. She would never master the knack of behaving as if servants were invisible, she decided.

Mathiaz downed most of the drink in one swallow and set the glass aside. "Why didn't you tell me you were involved in the explosion at the Treasury?"

Braced to have him ask her why she had walked out on him, she stared at him in bewilderment. "What?"

"You heard me. You were there, weren't you?"

She forced her head up and met his accusing gaze. No point denying what he had obviously remembered for himself. "I told you I was jogging past when it happened."

The baron's unrelenting look bored into her. "Not jogging past, at the scene. You were doing something, reaching for something. What was it? What were you doing, seconds before the bomb went off?"

If she told him the truth, he would know her deepest secret, how much she loved him, she thought feeling panic threaten to paralyze her. She managed a stiff shake of her head. "Please don't ask me."

"I am asking you, and I expect an answer." His expression hardened. "You're one of the conspirators, aren't you?"

How could he think such a thing? She felt tears start and blinked hard. "I had nothing to do with setting the bomb, I swear. You have to believe me."

"I wish I could."

Her thoughts reeled. She had never dreamed that Mathiaz would reach such a conclusion. She couldn't believe how deeply his suspicion hurt. The tragedy was, he was right, she had been more involved in the bomb scene than she had allowed him to know, but not as a conspirator.

He strode to the door and opened it, barking an order to the guard outside. Moments later, two members of the RPD came in, looking to the baron for further instructions. Jacinta recognized both officers as they stood at stone-faced attention in front of Mathiaz.

"Take Ms. Newnham to her suite and post a guard on her door."

The officers stationed themselves on either side of Jacinta. "You don't have to do this," she appealed.

The baron's mouth thinned. "You leave me no choice. I'm ordering you placed under house arrest until you're prepared to tell me what you were doing at the Treasury."

Jacinta glanced at Lyons whose back was to them. Should she tell Mathiaz that she had seen the equerry with Zenio's double earlier? Mathiaz would think she was stalling, trying to excuse herself. And what about Lyons himself? What was his part in all this? Until she had more to go on, Jacinta's sixth sense told her not to let the equerry know he'd been spotted.

Jacinta gave a slight shake of her head. "I have nothing more to say."

At her hesitation, hope had flared in Mathiaz's expression. Now Jacinta saw it fade. "Take her to her suite."

Her heart felt as if it was about to break as she was led away, the doors closing between her and Mathiaz, perhaps for the last time.

Chapter Eleven

The apartment that had seemed so luxurious felt distinctly limiting with a guard on the door. Jacinta had never liked being confined. Now she prowled the suite of rooms like a restless tiger, her thoughts churning.

It was late. She should go to bed. Tomorrow, without Lyons being present, she would tell Mathiaz and the police what she had seen. Once or twice, she could have imagined seeing a man who looked like Zenio in the palace grounds, but three times was stretching coincidence. The police would have to investigate.

Or they might decide she had invented the sightings to conceal an agenda of her own. She slammed one fist into the palm of the other. She needed proof that Zenio had a double, then they would have to believe her.

Mathiaz would have to believe her.

The disappointment in his expression as she was led away under guard haunted her. She didn't blame him for being suspicious. All the pieces fit, according to the memories he had recovered. She *had* been close to the bomb seconds before it exploded. For all he knew she could have been trying to detonate it.

The baron wasn't to know she'd hurled the device into the ornamental pond in front of the Treasury. Instead of sinking quickly, the device had skimmed over the surface, exploding with enough force to injure Mathiaz, and spear a shard of shrapnel into her forearm. No wonder she'd never made her local baseball team, she thought. Never could throw for peanuts.

She rubbed the healed injury absentmindedly, trying not to think of the damage the bomb could have caused if she hadn't thrown it as far as she had. They were alive. She would be better occupied trying to work out how she could be seeing Zenio in two places at once.

"I wish there were two of me." Shelley's words reverberated through Jacinta's memory with the force of the bomb itself. That had to be the explanation. There were two Zenios—a double, a brother, she didn't know which yet. He was the key.

His freedom to visit the palace grounds suggested he had a contact on the inside. Barrett Lyons? Without evidence that a double existed, accusing Lyons would get her nowhere. She had to get proof.

She stopped prowling and considered her options. Mathiaz had posted guards outside her door, but not on the balcony off her living room. She doubted whether the rest of the RPD knew about her house arrest yet, so even if they saw her in the grounds, her movements wouldn't arouse interest.

She was halfway to the balcony before she remembered that her outfit wasn't the most practical garment for investigative work. On the other hand, knots of people still strolled about, talking, laughing and enjoying the last of the evening. Dressed as she was, she could mingle easily with them.

Her wrap was still in Mathiaz's salon, so she bundled her purse and gun inside a hooded black wool cape and dropped them over the balustrade to the bushes below, before jumping after them.

Retrieving the items, she swirled the cape around her shoulders, glad of its warmth as the night cooled. A survey of the grounds revealed no sign of the man she'd seen with Barrett Lyons.

A group of visitors was heading for the main entrance so she tagged along with them, mentally thanking Mathiaz for giving her the idea.

The guards at the gates were on alert for possible intruders, but not for anyone going out. They barely glanced at her group. As soon as they cleared the lights pooling around the gates, she dropped back, letting the others continue to the nearby car park. All she needed now was a plan.

"Need a lift? We're going back to Perla."

She jumped as a light colored car pulled out near her. The driver was one of the group she'd been shadowing. Two women got into the back, chattering about their evening.

Jacinta thought fast. "If it's no trouble? I seem to have lost my date in the crowd."

"Sure, hop in."

They were American tourists, she discovered on the way to the city. She kept revelations about herself to a minimum.

"Where do you want to be dropped off?" the driver asked.

She gave the name of Zenio's street. If he was on Nuee, as he was supposed to be, she could look around without being disturbed. She waited until her new friends drove away, then pulled the hood of her cape up. Zenio's house was a few doors away. A light shone inside, but might have been left on for security.

Or not.

Her suspicion grew as the front door opened and a man stepped out, lighting a cigarette. Recognizing him, Jacinta imagined Zenio's wife nagging him for smoking when they had a new baby. She adjusted her hood so it concealed most of her face, then started walking. In the glow of the cigarette, the man looked startled at her approach.

Pitching her voice low, she said, "Andre darling. I'm so glad to see you."

"What in the devil..."

"It's me, Susie." If she was wrong and he *was* Andre, she was in big trouble.

"Whoever you are, you've got the wrong man."

She had the right man, he just didn't know it.

She projected hurt feelings into her tone. "Don't say you've forgotten me already, Andre, after working alongside me in the prison kitchen for three months. You promised we'd be together when you got out, but you haven't called once."

The man ground the cigarette out underfoot. "I don't know you, and I'm not Andre."

Adding a whiny touch, she said, "Stop it, Andre. You're scaring me."

The man's sigh whistled between them. "I don't know what my brother promised you, lady, but he's a family man with responsibilities."

Bingo. She controlled her excitement and said plaintively, "He's married?"

"I gather he didn't tell you?"

She shook her head. ''He didn't mention no brother, neither. You sure look like him.''

''I can't help that.'' The man reached a hand inside his jacket. She braced herself until he withdrew a fat wallet. ''How much?''

''I don't want money, I want to see Andre.''

''He doesn't want to see you.'' He peeled some bills out of the wallet and stuffed them into her hand. ''Find yourself another man who doesn't have a wife and a new baby.''

Sniffling for effect, she closed her hand around the bills, and hunched her shoulders as she turned away. Inwardly she was celebrating. She kept her posture downcast until she was out of sight of Zenio's house, then straightened and hailed a cab, letting Zenio's brother pay for it.

The ID in her purse got her back into Château Valmont without challenge. Climbing the balcony back into her suite was harder than jumping out. She was breathing hard by the time she stepped into the bedroom and threw the cape and purse onto a chair.

Night-blind, she blinked when the lights snapped on. Mathiaz was lounging on the bed, his back against the ornately carved headboard and his hand resting on the remote switch by the bedside. He still had on the dark pants and white shirt he'd worn to the fireworks. With his hair mussed as if he'd combed it with his fingers, he looked regal but untamed, Attila the Hun in black tie.

''Did you enjoy your outing?'' he said with deceptive softness.

Slowly she came up out of the crouch she'd instinctively dropped into. ''You could get yourself killed surprising me that way, Baron.''

His eyebrows arched. ''No explanation? No apologies?''

''Why should I apologize?''

''For breaking out of house arrest.''

''I had a good reason.''

He swung his long legs over the side of the bed and perched on the edge. ''I can't wait to hear it.''

His chilly tone said he didn't expect to believe her anyway. ''You really think I'm involved in setting the bomb, don't you?'' she asked.

''I saw you at the scene. Without an explanation, what else am I supposed to think?''

You're supposed to trust me, she thought in despair. Out loud, she said, ''I didn't want to say anything in front of Barrett Lyons, but I'm sure he's involved in this somehow. During the concert, I saw him talking to a man who looked exactly like Andre Zenio.''

Mathiaz padded closer. ''Lyons has served the royal family for decades. And we both saw this morning's police report placing Zenio on Nuee.''

''But not his twin brother.''

That stopped the baron, she noticed, although not for long. ''The RPD would have turned up a twin brother when they checked Zenio's background before he was originally hired, and later during the stalking investigation.''

''Not if there's no record of a twin. After seeing Zenio where he couldn't be, I decided to check. Legally the twin doesn't exist, even thought I met him myself tonight.''

''You could have invented him to clear your name.''

His accusation felt like an arrow to her heart. ''You really think I'm capable of that?''

His hands dropped to her shoulders as if he could

barely stop himself from shaking her. "You won't tell me what went on between us in the last year, and you won't explain why you were near the bomb moments before it exploded. Is it any wonder I'm suspicious?"

At his touch, a shudder gripped her. "Think what you like about me, but tell the police to check out the twin brother. They'll find him at Zenio's address in Perla."

"Assuming Zenio has a twin."

She winced at the skepticism lacing his voice. "Naturally," she agreed bitterly.

"What would he gain from assassinating me?"

She spread her hands, wishing the baron wouldn't stand so close, making it hard to think straight. "Political advantage? Revenge because you had his brother jailed? Notoriety? People like him have motives the rest of us can't imagine."

"You're doing a pretty fair job."

Because she was an accomplice, according to the baron. "If you're so suspicious of me, why don't you call the police and have me thrown in jail?" she snapped.

His mouth thinned. "I considered it after I came here to talk some sense into you, and found you'd gone."

He had come to talk. So he wasn't as convinced of her culpability as he wanted to be. More gratified than she should be, she lifted her head. "Why didn't you have me arrested?"

His gaze darkened. "In spite of your evasiveness, I don't think you belong behind bars."

That was a start. "You don't think I'm innocent, either?"

"I think you're innocent of trying to harm me, Jac."

She felt herself flush and looked away. "I would never willingly hurt you, Baron."

He heard what she didn't say, and touched a hand to the back of her heated cheek. "What about unwillingly?"

She sensed him circling her fear like a wolf scenting prey, and drew back mentally, since her feet felt as if they were anchored to the floor. "I'm not sure what you mean."

"There's a reason you don't want me getting too close to you." She worked at keeping her breathing even as he asked, "Are you married?"

The question was so far off base that she almost laughed with relief, until she saw that he was serious. Tempted to say yes and end this, she couldn't force the lie past her lips. On a gusting sigh, she said, "I'm not married. Never have been." Quite possibly never would be. "The background check the police did before I was hired would have told you that."

"Checks don't always reveal the whole story."

They hadn't in Zenio's case, she knew. "They weren't wrong about that. But I don't see ..."

Mathiaz cut her off by claiming her mouth in a long, deep kiss that left her reeling. She felt herself slipping, and didn't resist as he pulled her against him, answering his kiss from the depths of her own need.

She felt his fingers tangle in her hair and brought her hands up, linking them around his neck to pull him close. Sensations washed over her, glorious and confusing. She felt greedy with wanting him. She also sensed the shadow beasts of fear stalking her.

Like a pack of wolves, the nameless terrors hovered around the fringes of her awareness, warning her that harm could befall him if she let herself get too close.

Resisting the baseless terror, she clung to him, refusing to let fear win. This time she would not let her demons drive her away. Tremors ripped through her as desire to belong to Mathiaz warred with the powerful urge to turn and run.

Mathiaz skimmed his hands down her trembling body, reading her tremors as desire and responding out of some wellspring of his own. The wanting grew until it fevered her blood, blanking out all thought. She felt dizzy, held up by his skillful hands and demanding mouth.

Disoriented, she barely felt him unzip her halter top until a slight breeze feathered her heated skin as the silky fabric slithered to her waist. Mathiaz's touch replaced the fabric, clothing her in caresses that drove her to the brink of reason.

As her head fell back, Mathiaz felt her shudder and gloried in his effect on her. Her eyes were heavy-lidded, dark as smoke. Beautiful. He could barely think around the fast beating of his heart and the fever she fired in his blood.

He didn't have to think. She wanted him. He wanted her. What else mattered?

Answers.

The pounding in his head almost split his skull. Pain and the powerful need to know hammered at him. To know her? Yes. He wanted to possess her so much that his loins ached and his head swam. It was the other knowing—who she was to the depths of her soul, and what they had once meant to each other—that he sought.

Breathing shallowly, he buried his face in the curve of her neck. The womanly scent of her filled him, and the softness of her breasts molded against him, pushing him to the limits of his control.

Words of love hovered on his lips but instinct kept him silent. Some sense of being here before. Of frightening her away with those same words.

A memory?

She moaned softly, moving against his straining erection until the last vestiges of his restraint began to slip. Like a floodgate opening, images blurred through his mind almost too fast to absorb. He resisted the urge to fight, and let them come, although the pain dulled his desire. Blessed pain, giving him back the memory of their last year together.

His knees sagged and a blinding headache sang in his temples, but he didn't care. The mental storm passed quickly, leaving him feeling taller, stronger, reborn. He knew everything. Remembered everything.

Along with a year's worth of memories, relief flooded through him. Jacinta wasn't responsible for the bomb. She had tried to save him from it. As he got out of his car, he had seen her throw something toward the lake seconds before an explosion blanked everything out.

As his mind cleared, he also knew that the tremors he could feel gripping Jacinta were not untamed desire. He remembered that she had reacted like this after he first told her he loved her, before packing and leaving.

This time he was determined to find out what was wrong. "What's the matter?" he asked, caressing her brow and finding her now burning with fever.

"Nothing," she said, but he noted that her teeth clenched with the effort to stop them chattering.

He ripped the covering off the bed and draped it around them both. "You're ill."

"I'm all right." She shivered again.

"Something *is* wrong. I'll call a doctor."

He tried to release her but she burrowed closer. "Don't go, just hold me. That's all I need. Hold me, Mathiaz. Never let me go."

In the tent he'd made for them, holding her was easy.

The hard part was not progressing to the next step, which he desperately wanted to do. With the bed only a few steps away, he wanted to gather her into his arms, carry her to the bed and sheathe himself so deeply inside her that they would both be lost forever.

Her mouth on his told him she wanted the same thing. But her kiss held a frenetic quality that worried him. She seemed torn between panic and desire. Now he knew they'd played this scene out once before, he desperately wanted the outcome to be different this time.

The hands she slid over his body felt moist. He trapped her hands between his, feeling her shudder. She arched closer but he kept their hands between them, creating a distance only he knew how much he needed if he was to have any chance of making this work.

Telling her he had recovered his memory wasn't an option. She wouldn't leave while she thought he needed her, so he had to keep her in the dark for now. Playing the invalid a while longer wouldn't hurt him while he used his recovered knowledge of their relationship to change the future if such were possible. He needed to believe so.

Slowly, slowly, he commanded himself, aware of the throbbing in his loins threatening his vow of restraint. Holding her in his arms, smelling her seductive scent and feeling the litheness of her against him, gnawed at his will like a wild animal.

He fought the desire tearing through him. Until he knew why she'd run from him the last time, he couldn't permit himself to yield to desire. He cursed his memory for not including that detail. Obviously he had never known the why of it. This time he was determined that he should.

She tried to free herself, making a mew of objection deep in her throat when he held fast. "Mathiaz..."

"First, I need to know that you want me."

"Do you have to ask?" She sounded breathless.

He couldn't mistake the urgency between them when his body felt like a team of horses he could barely control. He made himself kiss her gently, feeling the horses pull so hard on the reins that they almost got away from him. He swallowed with difficulty, aware that more was at stake here than his own desires. "I believe you want me, but you're afraid for some reason."

She stiffened, her anxious body language telling him he was getting close. "Why should I be afraid?"

Still swathed in the blanket, he pulled her down with him on to the edge of the bed, but for comfort rather than seduction. However much he wanted her, and he had never wanted a woman more, there was a barrier to be broken down before their lovemaking could be as mutual as he desired. "Why don't you tell me?"

Jacinta squirmed against his hold, the phobia threatening to win as Mathiaz persisted in dragging it out into the open. She had felt fevered with wanting him. In that state, she was sure she could have subdued her demons enough to allow him to make love to her. He shouldn't have stopped.

Yes, he should. When they made love, he didn't want her to be afraid. He wanted her to be as willing as he was, she understood. In the closeness of the blanket tent he'd created around them, she couldn't help being aware of his arousal. Yet he'd held back for her sake. Deeply touched, she released a sigh of resignation. His strength was a two-edged sword he was going to apply to getting the truth from her.

Maybe it was time.

"When I was much younger, I loved a man." Feeling his stirring of objection, she added quickly, "We were teenagers, so in love I thought we'd invented the condition. We planned to marry as soon as we finished school."

He lifted her trapped hands to his mouth and kissed her fingertips. "Go on."

She licked parched lips. "I need a glass of water."

He shook his head. "You need to talk. You were in love."

"His name was Colin. We were driving home from a dance late one night when we got a flat. Colin was changing the tire when a carload of drunken teenagers stopped beside us."

She was rigid with tension now. She tried to order herself to relax. His closeness helped, although it inflamed her at the same time. She searched for the words. "They taunted us, started touching me. Colin tried to defend me and they..."

He stroked her hair. "It's all right."

She lifted blazing eyes to him. "It's not all right. One of them struck Colin with a tire iron. They killed him."

Her voice broke on the last words and Mathiaz's wrapped his arms around her, rocking her soothingly. "I can't possibly know how you feel. Having the man you loved murdered in front of you—" He broke off, imagining more vividly than he wanted to. How much worse for her, to have to deal with the reality.

When he looked at her again, his eyes glittered with a terrible fierceness, as if he would take on the murderers himself for her sake. His voice vibrated with controlled rage as he asked, "Did they attack you? Is that why you're so afraid of intimacy now?"

"I wish it was that simple." Her tone came out harsh,

brittle. He wanted to know it all, she told herself. "They would have done, but the police came along just in time. The men were arrested. My testimony sent them to jail for Colin's murder."

"Anyone would be scarred by such an experience."

"You don't understand. I wasn't scarred. I was… warped. Every time I get too close to someone, I'm swamped by a phobia that something terrible will happen to them." To you, she thought but didn't say.

He heard her anyway and his hold tightened. "Maybe you should follow the advice you gave me, and see a counselor."

She gave a hollow laugh. "Do you think I haven't tried that? Over the years I've tried shrinks, pills, even hypnosis. None of them made any difference so I gave them all up and resigned myself to living with the problem."

"Living without love," he supplied. "A bleak solution."

"It worked until now."

"And now?"

"You complicated everything."

He cupped her face in his hands. "Life is complicated, Jac."

She shivered. "But it doesn't scare the hell out of you, the way it does me."

He shook his head, denying the assertion. "I've seen you in tight situations. You've never shown any fear."

"Ironic, isn't it? I can wade into a fight, shoot bull's-eyes one after another, without turning a hair. Yet right now, I'm scared to death."

"I don't want you to be scared of me," he said softly.

How to tell him he exhilarated her even as the closeness terrified her? She ached with wanting him. She felt her eyes become wild, the blanket feeling like a strait-jacket. Her breathing quickened. "I can't talk about this any more."

He allowed the blanket to slip off her shoulders, watching her as she stood up and adjusted her clothes, then began to pace. "Running away isn't going to heal you."

She whirled to face him. "Neither are doctors, medications or talking. Don't you understand? The only solution is for me to keep my emotional distance. It's the only way I can function. It isn't so bad, really." Said often enough, she might convince herself.

He stood up, letting the blanket fall away. Dear heaven, he was magnificent, she thought, more conflicted than she had ever been.

"There isn't much of the night left. We'll talk about this again tomorrow," he said.

Disappointment swept through her. "Then I'm still under house arrest?"

He strode to the window and looked out. The first blush of dawn was already staining the sky. "If I say no, what will you do?"

The only thing she could do. "Return to Perla. Tell the RPD they'll have to arrange a replacement bodyguard for you." The prospect would kill her, but she knew better than to try to stay.

He spun to face her. "I don't want a replacement. I want you."

"Even though you think I'm involved in the bombing?"

He straightened his shoulders. "You gave me your word you had nothing to do with setting the bomb."

"Then you believe me?"

Relief swept through her as he nodded acceptance.

"Even about the twin brother. I'll have the police check that out. In the meantime, I need your word on something else."

Fresh tension threaded through her and she looked at him sharply, guessing what he had in mind. "Please don't do this, Baron."

"I must, for both our sakes. I want your promise to remain in my service for a few more days."

"What will that achieve? Now you know my story, you must know I'm not much use to you as I am."

"On the contrary, I feel we're finally getting somewhere."

"You can't change what I am," she insisted. "Why don't you let me go?"

The gaze he leveled at her was dark with desire, as dark as her own must be, she thought. "Because I don't want to," he said, "and I don't believe you really want to go."

He'd read that right, she thought on a sickening wave of apprehension. "Is this what they call aversion therapy?"

A slight smile lightened his expression. "As long as your aversion isn't to me."

Feelings she didn't know how to name swirled through her, but aversion wasn't among them. For the first time, she dared to hope. "I'll be here in the morning," she promised, knowing that whatever demons she had to fight, she would do it rather than break her word to him.

Hearing the conviction in her voice, he smiled more warmly. "I'll dismiss the guards on my way out."

"Thank you."

His face grew grave. "You might be thanking me too soon. Tomorrow, the real work starts." He was gone before she could ask him to explain.

Chapter Twelve

Next morning, she was far from pleased when she found out what he had in mind.

"Since you insist you still want me as your bodyguard, I can't sanction a visit to the Treasury so soon," she said after hearing what he intended to do.

He nodded as if her objection had been anticipated. "I'm not asking your permission. We're going this afternoon."

Ice slid down her spine. "We?"

"You're coming with me."

They were breakfasting together at his villa, a habit they'd established since he came home from the hospital. At first she had argued that as an employee she should eat in her suite, or with the other staff in their dining room, but he had insisted he wanted her company.

Usually she looked forward to spending the hour with him, and had even started to enjoy being waited upon by the servants.

Not today.

She dumped two teaspoons of sugar into her coffee and stirred ferociously, needing the energy after such a short night. He couldn't mean to go through with this? "Until the bomber is caught, what you propose is asking for trouble," she protested.

He cradled his cup in two hands, looking at her through the curls of steam. The translucent china embossed with the royal crest looked absurdly delicate in his masculine grasp. Remembering how seductively those same hands had glided over her skin in the early hours of the morning, she had a struggle to stay focused.

"You've heard the saying about the best defense being a good offense?" he observed.

She felt alarm light her gaze. "You *want* someone to try something?"

He gestured with the cup. "It's the only way I'm going to get some answers."

She refrained from pointing out that answers of the sort he wanted frequently came at a price. "What does the RPD think of your plan?"

He waited while a maid placed a plate of cinnamon-dusted French toast in front of him and served Jacinta her usual breakfast of fresh and dried fruit with yogurt, before saying, "I haven't asked them."

"You do intend to take a squad with you?" With sinking heart, she guessed what his answer was going to be.

"Not this time. My bodyguard can take care of me."

"Like I did the last time."

He heard the bitterness she couldn't keep out of her tone, and frowned his impatience. "You weren't in my service at the time of the bombing."

"I should have been." Would have been if she hadn't allowed her demons to drive them apart.

He dismissed her attempted *mea culpa* with a gesture. "You'll be at my side this time, and that's what matters."

She pushed a slice of papaya around the plate, her appetite gone. "I'm surprised you're willing to rely on me after what I told you last night."

He cut his French toast with care. "Your revelation hasn't changed my faith in you, Jac. If anything, I respect you all the more for knowing what a battle you've had to get where you are today."

"Not exactly the way I expected success to come," she said, "considering I started out planning to be a kindergarten teacher."

His expression softened. "I can picture you throwing recalcitrant four-year-olds over your shoulder."

She was forced to smile, too. "Putting them in a headlock is the worst part, but sometimes it's the only way to get them to eat their vegetables."

"Works for me." He ate in silence for a few minutes, then said, "I think you'd be good with children."

She didn't want to think about children right now, with the memory of his caresses so fresh in her mind. "I make a pretty fair aunt. My sister, Debbie, may not agree. She says I spoil her brood."

"How many children does she have?"

She realized that her family's visit to Carramer had taken place during the time they had been apart. "Three. There's baby Ryan, seven-year-old Christie and ten-year-old Matthew." Talking about them made her aware of how much she missed her family. Letters and phone calls were only a partial substitute.

Mathiaz pushed his plate away and rested his chin on one hand. "I'd like to meet them."

"Mom and Dad don't like taking time away from the

farm, but my sister and her family came for a vacation a few months ago.'' She hadn't told them about Mathiaz, not wanting the third-degree from Debbie. Bad enough to be on the receiving end of hints about what a cute page boy Ryan would make and how sweet Christie would look as a bridesmaid. Jacinta hadn't wanted to let Debbie think there was any chance of a candidate for groom when there wasn't.

As the thought of a wedding lingered in her mind, Jacinta felt her throat go dry and gulped orange juice. A change of subject was called for so she said briskly, ''How do you intend to handle your visit to the Treasury?''

''I'm going to finish what the bomb interrupted, having Antoinette's Wedding Ring revalued. I told Barrett Lyons to arrange for the royal valuer to meet us there at two this afternoon.''

Her startled gaze flashed to him. ''You told Barrett Lyons? Even though he might be...''

''Precisely.'' He cut across her.

''You're hoping to smoke him out, make him betray himself,'' she observed, not liking the idea. ''I hope you know what you're doing, Baron.''

He leveled a reassuring look at her. ''Trust me.''

''It's Zenio's twin brother I don't trust.'' Until they knew where he fitted in, she wouldn't get much peace.

Mathiaz drained his coffee cup and stood up. ''He won't be a problem. I'll have the police pick him up before we leave for the Treasury.'' He consulted his watch. ''I have a cabinet meeting at ten. Time for a workout before then.''

She concealed her anxiety behind a smile. ''Aren't you concerned I'll throw you over my shoulder?''

He looked affronted. "As I recall, you were the one who got thrown when we worked out the last time."

And several other times. No matter how she tried to tell herself she had been going easy on him, she knew he outmatched her on several levels. One of them was emotional, as she had learned last night to her cost.

He grinned at her. "You can always pretend I'm four-year-old Ryan."

Impossible to do when the baron's every move screamed full-grown male at her. "I'll settle for a walk on the beach instead," she said, choosing discretion over valor. He didn't offer to join her and she wondered if he'd made the same choice.

On the way back to her suite, her thoughts were uneasy. Not only the Treasury visit bothered her, she realized as she returned to her bedroom to change into shorts and a T-shirt for her walk. Something else nagged at her. When had she told Mathiaz how old Ryan was?

The Treasury Building was a popular tourist destination in Perla, housing as it did the Valmont Crown Jewels. Jacinta had gone to see them soon after moving to the province, and had been impressed by both the display, and the building where it was housed.

Once home to the first prince of Valmont, the rose granite building was Moorish in style, with high, plantation ceilings and rooms of massive proportions, paneled in sandalwood. In the center of the main lobby was an enormous circular aquarium filled with luminescent tropical fish and coral.

Outside, carved columns supported a substantial port cochere facing an ornamental lake, a monument to the past ruler. A road separated the precinct from the white sands of Diamond Beach, itself buffered from the city activity by a grassy lawn and ancient shade trees. Like the majority of Perla residents, she had played volleyball on the sands, jogged along the shady paths and swum in the tranquil blue waters of the bay. That was before the area came to represent the nightmare of Mathiaz's injury and memory loss.

As a result, relaxation was far from her mind as Mathiaz's limousine brought them to a private side entrance away from the public lobby. She was wearing a cream linen pantsuit and cerise silk blouse to conceal the reassuring bulk of her gun in the shoulder holster. She hoped she wouldn't need to use it.

Mathiaz walked up the steps and nodded as a guard came to attention and saluted. Walking beside the baron, her eyes darting everywhere, Jacinta couldn't help reliving the last time, when his confident approach to this same place had ended in the hideous roar of an explosion and the terrifying sight of him lying injured on the marble floor.

She rubbed her forearm, recalling the burn she had collected when the bomb had exploded over the pond. The injury had healed but not her memory of that day which was still enough to awaken her, sweating, from a deep sleep.

She forced the memory away and applied herself to her job. This time she saw no signs of anything other than normal activity. She should be thankful Mathiaz had allowed the police to check out the area in advance, but wished he had agreed to bring along more security.

As if reading her thoughts, he gave her a reassuring look that only made the blood sing more loudly in her head. Something was going to go wrong. She could feel it. Or was it her own concern for the baron's safety she could feel? She couldn't tell anymore.

She was conscious of his footsteps echoing on the marble floor as they were shown into the inner chamber where the royal family conducted their private business within the Treasury. She tensed, seeing Barrett Lyons already there, seated at a long mahogany conference table, a leather covered box in front of him. He got to his feet.

The aide looked distressed. ''I'm afraid Antoinette's Wedding Ring is nowhere to be found, Lord Montravel. I've conducted a thorough search of the vault.''

Mathiaz's face showed none of the fury he must be feeling. ''You assured me it was accounted for after the explosion.''

Lyons nodded. ''The ring has not been on public display since then, and was believed to be safely in the vault.''

''Who has accessed this chamber since the explosion?''

Lyons shifted restively. ''Before today, only Ms. Newnham.''

Mathiaz swung to face her but directed his question to his equerry. ''When was this?''

''Right after the explosion, sir. She insisted on seeing that the ring was intact before following you to the hospital.''

Nightmarish images of that day flashed through her mind. ''That's an outright lie.''

''You were at the scene,'' Mathiaz insisted.

She gave a taut nod. ''I've never denied that, but I didn't know you were here to see the ring.'' She didn't add that Mathiaz's survival had been the only thing on her mind. It had never occurred to her to wonder what he was doing at the Treasury. ''Lyons is trying to set me up, and I'd like to know why,'' she said.

"So would I."

The baron's quiet statement drew his aide up short. "After all my years of service, surely you wouldn't believe her word over mine, Lord Montravel?"

"Once, I wouldn't have hesitated. But something's changed. Care to tell us what, Barrett?"

Mathiaz's use of his first name startled the other man, she saw, and was amazed to see his eyes gleam with moisture. He blinked hard. "I don't know what you mean."

"I think you do. I also think you know where the ring is."

Her astonishment must have been as obvious as Lyons's, she thought, as the equerry's hand went to his jacket. He pulled it back but too late. His instinctive movement had betrayed him. His face turned ashen. "How did you know?"

"I was guessing until your reaction gave you away." Mathiaz said on a note of satisfaction.

"Shall I search him, Baron?" Jacinta moved purposefully closer to Lyons but before Mathiaz could answer, the other man sagged against the conference table.

"There's no need. The ring is here."

She braced herself as he reached inside his jacket, but when he pulled his hand out he had only the gem in his palm. His hand shook as he gave the ring to the baron.

Mathiaz inspected the ring closely. "Not a bad copy, but a copy, nonetheless."

Jacinta's confusion grew as Lyons nodded wearily. "As you've evidently guessed, I removed the real one and replaced it with the copy."

Had Lyons tried to cover his tracks with the explosion? "Why did you steal the ring in the first place?" she asked.

"I had no choice. I was being blackmailed."

Mentally she added the last piece to the puzzle. "By Andre Zenio, or his twin brother?"

Lyons looked startled, then seemed to collapse in on himself. "You know about Paul?"

"So it would seem," a voice contributed. With Andre on Nuee, he had to be Paul Zenio. She noticed that he positioned himself directly under the security camera. Not an amateur at criminal activity, she would have concluded, even without the automatic pistol he held on them.

He must have somehow eluded the police Mathiaz had sent to pick him up. She felt her heart pound as her worst nightmare became reality. Mathiaz was in danger and there was nothing she could do to protect him. The gun nestling against her shoulder was useless. By the time she could draw, Zenio could have gunned Mathiaz down in cold blood.

"How did you get in here?" the baron demanded.

"When my uncle told me about your appointment with the royal valuer, I arranged a car accident, relieved the real valuer of his identification without him noticing, and took his place. He's still at the scene, waiting for the police to arrive."

"You may have managed to get in here successfully, but getting out won't be so easy," the baron said.

Jacinta saw Paul Zenio glance at her. "I think it will, in the right company." So he intended to take her hostage. Better her than the baron, she thought, her mind racing through possibilities. Every one she could think of put Mathiaz at greater risk.

"I don't intend to leave empty-handed, either," Zenio added.

Lyons wrung his hands. "Isn't the ring enough for you?"

"I have an expensive lifestyle."

"Were you the one who stalked Lord Montravel?" she asked.

Zenio shook his head. "That really was Andre. He repented after he went to jail, but his record came in handy when I came back to Carramer. I could do anything I wanted knowing he would be blamed."

Keep him talking, she thought. Buy time for the real valuer to show up, or for her to figure a way out of this. "Why is there no record of Andre having a twin?"

"Our father mixed up the paperwork and only registered one birth: Andre Paul Zenio, instead of Andre *and* Paul. Legally, I don't exist," Paul added. "After we were born, our folks' marriage turned sour. With no divorce in Carramer, my father took me with him and rattled around the Pacific, not always on the side of the law, until he died of a tropical fever, leaving me to make my own way."

She heard the resentment in his voice. "So you decided to come back and make trouble here."

"My brother had written to me about his highly placed patron. I decided to fool Lyons into thinking I was Andre, out on parole for good behavior."

Lyons spoke tiredly. "I was so surprised to see him that I stupidly let him into my office. Before I discovered the truth, he had stolen money and valuables, threatening to have me blamed. Since Andre was still in jail and Paul technically didn't exist, no one would believe I wasn't the thief.

"When he demanded the ring, I had a copy made, hoping Paul would think it was genuine, but it didn't work. He planted the bomb as a diversion so I could switch the fake with the real ring. He promised me nobody would get hurt.''

''You should have known better than to trust a blackmailer,'' Mathiaz snapped.

''I know that now, and I would do anything to undo the harm caused to you. But all I could think about was buying Paul's silence to preserve my reputation.''

''I had to break into your château before he'd believe I meant business,'' Zenio said.

She rubbed her throat, remembering. ''You shouldn't have picked the night your brother's baby was born. He had a perfect alibi.''

Zenio frowned. ''Nobody expected his wife to go into early labor. It doesn't matter. You thought I was him, didn't you?''

Mathiaz planted his hands on his hips. ''You realize by confessing to us, you've lost your main advantage. You won't be invisible anymore. You may as well give this up.''

Zenio swung the pistol on Mathiaz, and Jacinta's heart stalled. She had known something would go terribly wrong if she allowed herself to love Mathiaz. Her mind tumbled back to the night when another man she loved was killed while she stood by impotently. Blackness fringed her vision. Her worst fears were being realized. The terror was happening all over again.

Desperately she wrenched her thoughts back to the present. This time she wasn't a teenager, and she had skills she hadn't possessed then. All she had to do was master her fear and use them. Mathiaz's life was at stake.

''Do you still have the ring, Paul?'' she asked, injecting a teasing lilt into her voice.

He swung the pistol to her, as she'd intended. ''What of it?''

"I can help you get out of here, for the right price."

She heard Mathiaz's breath catch. Good, his reaction would strengthen her hand.

Zenio looked skeptical. "You tried to stop the bomb going off. I was watching from the park and saw you grab it, but a group of tourists got in my way. I couldn't see what you did before it exploded."

She smiled, holding his attention. "You're wrong. You set the device too far away to do any real damage, so I moved it closer."

One glance at Mathiaz's appalled expression made her heart turn over. She prayed that he would know she was putting on an act. She returned her gaze to Zenio, afraid that if she looked at Mathiaz for too long she would give herself away.

Zenio's eyes narrowed. "Why would you help me?"

"Lyons must have told you I was sacked from my job as the baron's bodyguard a few months ago. You helped me to get even."

"But you still work for him."

She leaned toward him conspiratorially. "He actually gave me my job back because he thought I tried to save his life."

Zenio chuckled. "Amoral as well as brave. A lady after my own heart. Come over here. I still need a hostage, but if you play your cards right and don't give me any trouble, we may be able to work something out."

She'd thought he'd never ask. As soon as she was within striking distance, she lashed out with her foot, sending the gun flying. She followed the move by slashing her bladed hand across Zenio's throat. As the gunman reeled, choking, Mathiaz leaped on him, hauling him to his feet and twisting his arms up and behind him.

"A lady could get corrupted by language like yours,"

she told the swearing, struggling Zenio. Her blow to his throat had reduced him to a hoarse-voiced whisper, just as well given the obscenities he spat at her.

"For a minute there, I thought she had been, until I worked out what you were up to," Mathiaz said, his grin as wide as hers felt. "Good work, Jac."

The compliment triggered a fresh wave of crude language from Zenio until Mathiaz tightened his grip with painful effect. The gunman subsided into sullen silence.

Jacinta couldn't resist. She sashayed up to Zenio and said in a flirtatious voice, "Don't say you've forgotten me already, Andre, after working alongside me in the prison kitchen for three months. You promised we'd be together when you got out, but you haven't called once."

"It was you." The rest of Zenio's gravel-voiced response was unprintable, but she didn't care. Inwardly she was celebrating. She hadn't allowed her demons to beat her, and Mathiaz was alive as a result. She could risk letting herself love him after all. In the same breath she wondered if she had ever had a choice.

"Summon the guards," Mathiaz instructed. Jacinta was happy to comply.

Giving statements to the police took some time, but eventually Zenio was safely in custody and Lyons was freed on his own recognizance. A search warrant was being obtained for the Zenio home, and the police fully expected to recover Antoinette's wedding ring.

"Not a bad day's work," he said when they returned to his villa at Château Valmont. "Will you join me in a celebratory glass of champagne?"

She had felt like celebrating ever since realizing that

she could control her fears, and act in spite of them. ''I'd like that.''

He handed her a brimming goblet, and touched his own to hers. ''To a mission accomplished.''

She took a sip before lowering the glass. ''There's one mission we haven't accomplished yet. You still haven't recovered your memory of the last year.''

He gave her an enigmatic look. ''Are you sure about that?''

His comment about her nephew's age clicked into place. She knew she hadn't told him how old little Ryan was this time, yet he had known the child's age. She should have guessed the truth. ''When did you regain your memory?''

He looked away. ''It happened when we came close to making love.''

''So you didn't need me to tell you about my past, in order to know I wasn't one of the bombers. You'd already remembered everything.''

''You needed to talk,'' he said quietly. ''I'd already found out the bare facts after you walked out on me. I needed to know why you couldn't stay, when I knew you cared for me.''

She put the goblet down with exaggerated care, to avoid throwing it at him. ''You allowed that whole scene in the Treasury to unfold for my benefit.''

''I wanted to show you that history doesn't have to repeat itself. And to smoke out Lyons and Zenio's twin brother,'' he said almost as an afterthought.

She could hardly believe what she was hearing. ''You put your life at risk to prove a point to me?''

''More than a point. I want us to be together, Jac. The only way was to exorcise your demons, and we did that today.''

She kept her voice deceptively mild. ''This is where I say how grateful I am, and agree to be yours forever, right?''

He frowned at her. ''Do you have a problem with that?''

She struggled to keep her anger in check. ''I have a problem with being manipulated, especially for my own good. Last time I left because I have—used to have—a phobia about harm coming to any man I allowed myself to love. That fear was unreasonable. Now you expect me to live with the prospect of you doing something crazy on my behalf, just as you did today. I don't think I want to live with that particular worry. Thanks for the champagne.''

Mathiaz didn't like the finality he heard in her voice. ''That sounds suspiciously like another goodbye.''

''The threat to you ended today, so the RPD can take over protecting you. You have your memory back. You don't need me anymore.''

She walked out without giving him chance to tell her how very much he did.

Chapter Thirteen

Her apartment occupied the penthouse of a four-story building on a hill north of Perla, with a view all the way to Diamond Beach. She had bought and decorated the apartment out of the profits from the academy, choosing every item of furniture with all the care and pride of a first home owner.

When had the apartment started to feel like a prison?

The day she moved back after walking out of Mathiaz's life for the last time, she accepted. That had been two days ago, she thought as she put herself through a strenuous workout on the gym equipment she'd set up in one of the spare rooms.

Finding out that he had manipulated her to cure her of her phobia was unacceptable. Heaving weights over her head, she told herself he was royalty. He was used to running people's lives. She brought the weights back to their rest with a crash. She wasn't going to let him run hers.

She sat up, straddling the padded bench. Was that

what this was all about? She had told him she wasn't prepared to live with the risk that he might put himself in danger again. Was she really afraid of losing control of her life?

As Mathiaz's wife, Jacinta Newnham would cease to exist as an individual. She would be swallowed up by the powerful royal establishment and regurgitated as Baroness Montravel, with retainers, royal duties, who knew, even a bodyguard of her own.

She laughed out loud, imagining herself hiding behind a protector, but a nagging sense of discomfort told her that she was getting to the heart of her problem. Thanks to Mathiaz, the irrational fear that something might happen to him if she let herself love him was gone, so why was she still afraid to trust her future to him?

She showered and changed into jeans and a T-shirt, trying to relax, but the problem nagged at her. Unable to solve it, she threw herself onto the couch and picked up the remote. In the video player was a movie she'd hired the night before. *Moonlight* proclaimed the title on the cover lying next to her. The movie she and Mathiaz had never managed to watch right through.

Thinking of why, she felt herself color. Why had she rented that particular movie? The last thing she needed now was to wallow in sentiment for a couple of hours, getting more aroused than she was to start with.

She watched the movie anyway, finding tears rolling down her face when the hero told the heroine that he had no choice but to return to his wife, who was lying in a coma in the hospital. She would never awaken, but he wouldn't abandon her, although he loved the heroine with all his heart.

When the nitwit of a heroine told him she understood, Jacinta almost threw the remote at the set. "His wife won't even know he's there. You know, and can give him what he needs,'' she snapped at the unresponsive set. ''For goodness sake tell him so. Life is too short. Let him be a hero, but don't throw away what you could have together.''

She hit the pause button and stared at the frozen screen in astonishment. Who was she talking to, the heroine or herself? Herself, she decided, stopping the tape and jabbing at the off switch. It was time she and Mathiaz had a talk.

She was fated not to know how the movie ended, she thought as she headed for her front door. She swung it open and almost collided with a large male body. Her heart felt as if it was being squeezed in a vise. ''Mathiaz, what are you doing here?''

''Where are you rushing off to?'' he asked in the same moment.

They stared at one another. ''You first,'' he said gallantly.

''I was coming to see you.''

He looked confused but some of the darkness lifted from his expression. ''You were?''

''We have some unfinished business. Come with me.''

He didn't protest or ask for an explanation when she grabbed his hand and towed him to the elevator. He had a new minder, she noticed, seeing the tall, good-looking chauffeur lounging against Mathiaz's car. Jacinta was female enough to be glad he hadn't replaced her with another woman.

''We're only going across the park,'' she told the startled security man, pleased to see him get into the car and follow them at snail's pace, keeping his questions to himself.

When she stopped outside a tall building nestled

against the side of a real cliff, Mathiaz read the sign, sounding bemused. "The Cliff Center? Why do you want to go in here?"

"It's an indoor climbing gym. Ever been to one?"

"With so many natural climbs around Carramer, it never occurred to me."

"You can't always count on the weather, even in Carramer." Or on being able to conjure up a cliff in a hurry when you needed one, like now, she thought.

She was aware of her heart beating uncomfortably fast, and her hand in Mathiaz's was damp. She had never been a fan of climbing, usually preferring her workouts to be solo affairs. Climbing required too much dependence on another person, the very reason she wanted—no, needed—to do this now.

She had visited the center often enough for the owner, Mick Darcy, to know her. Mick looked startled, recognizing Mathiaz. "Baron Montravel, this is an unexpected pleasure. Had I been forewarned, I would have prepared a personal tour for you."

"This is purely a private visit. I don't want any fuss," Mathiaz assured him, with a glance at her. "My…friend thinks this is an experience we need to have."

She needed to have, she thought. She gritted her teeth before they could start chattering. She told herself she had to see this through if she was to have any chance of a future with Mathiaz. "Could we use the private chamber, Mick?" she asked.

He nodded. "It's set up for an advanced group who are due in this afternoon. You can use it in the meantime. The pitches are fairly steep. I'll come and give you a hand."

Mick's curiosity had nothing on Mathiaz's, she was aware as she shook her head. "I know the drill, so I'll take it from here. Will you make sure we're not disturbed?''

Mick nodded in deference to the baron. ''Of course. Delighted to have your patronage, Lord Montravel.''

''My pleasure,'' the baron said, adding in an undertone, ''I think.''

When they were alone in the private chamber, he looked up at the walls of artificial rock rising two stories high on three sides of the chamber. ''Would you mind telling me why you think I need climbing lessons? I've climbed all over the South Pacific.''

''You don't need the lesson, I do.''

She was glad he didn't press her for an explanation. He would have one soon enough, when she knew whether it was in her to trust him, to love him without reservation.

The wall she chose replicated part of the Staircase Tower. The original was a thirteen-hundred-foot quartzite rock spire that guarded Staircase Spur on the Carramer island of Nuee. The Tower, as it was better known, had challenged climbers for over a century. As Mick had warned, this section was for advanced climbers, but she had tackled it before successfully. That wasn't what she wanted to prove.

''You'll be my belayer,'' she told Mathiaz as she strapped herself into a climbing harness. He nodded. Her hands felt icy as she handed him the belay rope. In a real climb, the belayer would climb first and hold the belay rope in case the climber fell. In the indoor version, the rope was secured at the top of the climb. The belayer remained on the ground, braced to take the strain in case the climber slipped. Not for nothing was the belay line jokingly called the umbilical rope, she knew. In a crisis, it became a literal lifeline.

"Why are you doing this?" he asked, watching her prepare.

"I need to find out a few things about trust," she said, her voice husky.

He frowned. "You must know by now that you can trust me, Jac, if that's what this is about."

She pressed her closed fist against her chest. "Knowing it and believing it in here, are two different things. Today I realized I haven't really trusted anyone since Colin was murdered. I have to find out whether I can, before I'm any use to you—or myself."

He touched her cheek. "You don't have to prove anything to me. And as for the other, I won't let you fall."

She covered his hand with hers, feeling her self-doubt expand. She wanted to put her life in his hands not only today, but in the future, and she had to know if she could. Straightening her shoulders, she began to climb, aware that Mathiaz's grip on the rope was her only protection from falling.

Steadying her breathing she climbed upward, jamming her hands and feet into each elusive handhold until she was spread-eagled, her fingers aching from clinging to the rough-hewn surface.

Reaching the top of the first pitch, she stopped on an artificial rock ledge to rest—and to think. She was climbing well and knew she could reach the top easily.

The first time she'd tackled this wall, she'd nearly run out of steam halfway. Mick had been belaying her himself and had urged her to come down and climb the next pitch when she was fresh. She had continued on doggedly, preferring to work herself to exhaustion before she would put herself in his hands.

Never once in all the time she'd been climbing had she allowed her belayer to take over and help her down.

No matter what it cost her, she had made the climb up and down all by herself. For that reason, she restricted her climbing to indoor venues, knowing her refusal to trust others could put lives at risk in the real world.

"Are you okay?" Mathiaz called in concern.

"I'm fine."

"You realize the next pitch is twice as steep."

"I know." That wasn't what scared her. She knew she could manage the climb, but she didn't know if she could meet the tougher challenge—letting go and trusting him.

There was the problem. Like the last time, she was ready to force herself on beyond her endurance, rather than take the risk of trusting him.

"If you want to let go, I'm ready for you," Mathiaz said, reading her mind.

She wavered, then turned to the rock face, shutting out the fear-awakening thoughts. She placed her foot on a narrow nubbin of rock in front of her, jammed her fingers into a crevice at the limit of her reach, and started upward again.

Mathiaz was right. This face was far steeper, with handholds spaced so far apart that her muscles protested as she stretched for them. She shut the burning sensation out of her awareness. The top beckoned seductively only a few meters ahead.

Clinging to the face, she made herself stop. Two choices confronted her. She could continue climbing to a summit she already knew she could reach, and prove nothing to herself. Or she could step off into the air and let Mathiaz lower her to the ground.

She wanted to rage at the universe, at herself for taking on this absurd challenge, and at Mathiaz for his involvement. Why hadn't he stopped her? Accepted that she would never be the woman he wanted?

"You're not alone, Jac," Mathiaz said from below. "I'm here if you want to let go."

She had known all along that this wasn't about externals she couldn't control, such as the position of the hand and footholds, but about what was inside her, the invisible belay ropes of relationships that were there to keep her safe if only she would let herself use them. It was now or never.

"I'm coming down," she said.

Dragging in a shuddering breath that was half sob, she stepped off into the air, trusting Mathiaz to hold the rope tightly and break her fall. She knew a moment of stark terror then, amazingly, fear transmuted to a sense of lightness and freedom as he belayed her safely down to his side.

He helped her off with the harness and wrapped her in a tight embrace, brushing away the wetness staining her cheeks. "I didn't let you fall."

"No, you didn't." Her legs trembled and her arms ached but she felt as elated as if she had conquered a real mountain instead of her own fear. She had trusted Mathiaz and he hadn't let her down. She would never doubt him again, if he still wanted her, that was.

Her stomach fluttered as he lowered his mouth to hers, answering her unspoken question with a passion that touched her to the depths of her soul.

He lifted his head, his breath warm against her lips. "It means a lot to have your trust, Jac. I think I know how hard it was for you."

She shook her head. "In the end, it wasn't hard at all. Resisting was much harder. Trying to do everything myself.'' She chuckled. ''That's why I got so angry with you for that stunt you pulled at the Treasury.''

''Worked,'' he said, skimming his fingertips down her face.

She shuddered with longing but brought her head up. ''Next time you want to play therapist, I'd rather you did it with a couch instead of a gun.''

''There's an appealing idea.''

''I don't mean...''

He silenced her with another kiss. ''I do. The couch I have in mind doesn't involve therapy, unless it's the intimate kind with fantasies and lots of touching.''

''Sounds good to me.'' Unbelievably good. ''I suppose when you're royal, propriety dictates that you wait until you're married?''

His eyes gleamed. ''Is that a marriage proposal, Jacinta?''

She felt herself flush. ''I suppose it is.''

''Then I accept.'' He fished in his pocket and pulled out a velvet box. ''Just as well I brought this with me.''

She had wondered what had brought him to her door. ''What is it?''

''Open it.''

She found herself staring at a stunning ring in the shape of a winged heart set with flawless champagne diamonds. ''Antoinette's Wedding Ring,'' she said, stunned to have the heirloom in her hands. She had heard on the television news that the police had retrieved it from Zenio's household, along with enough other evidence to put Paul Zenio out of harm's way for a long time. Her eyes were wet as she looked at Mathiaz. ''It's beautiful.''

''Not yet.'' He took the ring out of the box and placed it on her wedding finger. ''*Now* it's beautiful.'' He lifted her chin. ‘‘The last two days without you have been pure hell. I came prepared to drag you back to Château Valmont if necessary, to make you understand how much I love you and need you at my side.’’

‘‘And I, you,’’ she assured him. Saying it got easier with practice, and she intended to get lots of practice. ‘‘There’s one more thing, Baron.’’

He mimed impatience. ‘‘More conditions?’’

‘‘You’ll like this one. I want to start a family as soon as possible.’’

He looked wickedly pleased. ‘‘We can start now, if you like.’’

She liked, but didn’t want to begin their married life with a royal scandal. ‘‘I mean after we’re married. Yesterday I handed over the running of the academy to Shelley, and I like being busy.’’

‘‘Children should do the trick,’’ he agreed. ‘‘Anything else?’’

She stuck her tongue firmly into her cheek. ‘‘If Baroness Montravel ever needs a bodyguard, I want a luscious male hunk.’’

‘‘You’ll get a hatchet-faced matron and like it,’’ he said sternly. ‘‘I know only too well what these bodyguards can get up to.’’

She stood on tiptoe to kiss him and reveled in the feel of his arms around her. ‘‘You didn’t object.’’

‘‘That was different. From now on, the only male guarding your beautiful body is going to be me.’’

She gave a silvery laugh. ‘‘I can live with that.’’ Forever, she thought, liking the idea more and more. She had never known the future to be so bright with promise.

Epilogue

"That was a fine speech you gave at dinner," Mathiaz told his younger brother, Eduard. Home on leave from the Carramer Royal Navy, Eduard looked tired but handsome in his commander's uniform. Not as handsome as Mathiaz, but close, Jacinta thought, knowing how prejudiced she was.

Eduard smiled. "It isn't every day I get to toast the health of my brother and his bride-to-be. Weren't you the one who said you'd never marry?"

Mathiaz had the grace to look abashed. "That was before I met Jacinta."

They were seated on the terrace of Mathiaz's villa, sharing a nightcap in the balmy spring night. The rest of the royal family had retired for the night, after sharing in a sumptuous banquet presided over by Prince Josquin to welcome Jacinta to their midst.

She still had trouble believing she was about to become a member of the Carramer royal family. Lady Jacinta, Baroness Montravel, she thought, glad that Mathiaz still called her Jac when they were alone. Keeping her feet on the ground was becoming increasingly difficult but he took the whole royal experience so much in stride that she was determined to learn from him.

She looked at the ring on her finger, marveling at what it represented. "You're the first woman to wear that ring since our grandmother," Eduard said, following her gaze. "Princess Antoinette would be pleased to see it being worn again in celebration of love instead of moldering in a display cabinet at the Treasury."

She raised her eyebrows. "Didn't Prince Henry's wife wear the ring?" Mathiaz's uncle, Prince Henry, the late ruler of Valmont Province, had left the ring to Mathiaz in his will so Jacinta had assumed it had belonged to Henry's wife.

"Princess Rose was half-nun," Mathiaz said with a laugh. "She hardly ever wore jewelry, and only the plainest clothes."

Poor Rose, Jacinta thought. "From what I've heard, Prince Henry was something of a tyrant, so maybe that was her way of escaping from his domination," she speculated.

The royal brothers laughed. Mathiaz said, "You could be right, although from what I recall of our aunt, she was happy enough in her own way."

"Not as happy as you two lovebirds," Eduard contributed. "You realize you have Prince Henry to thank for your happiness." In response to Jacinta's mystified look, he said, "If you hadn't inherited the ring, there would have been no conspiracy, Jacinta would never have returned as your bodyguard, and we wouldn't be celebrating your engagement tonight."

"True enough," Mathiaz agreed.

He looked at her with such love in his eyes that a

shiver of longing ran through Jacinta. How was she going to endure the weeks of preparation before they could be together? She understood that royal weddings took time to arrange, but she couldn't help being impatient. She forced her attention back to the conversation.

"We've discussed our plans, but you haven't mentioned what you intend to do with your accrued leave," Mathiaz said to his brother.

Eduard strolled to the balustrade and rested his forearms against it, looking out at the darkened gardens and the ocean beyond. "I plan to take the chopper and fly up to Tiga Falls Lodge. I haven't had chance to visit the place since Henry bequeathed it to me in his will."

It was left to Jacinta to ask, "Tiga Falls?"

"A lodge in a wilderness area about a hundred and fifty kilometers north of Perla," Mathiaz explained. "It always was one of Eduard's favorite places. After we're married, I'll take you there if it's all right with you, Eduard."

His brother turned to them. "You'll be welcome. Tiga Falls was once the ruler's hunting lodge. These days it's used as a retreat from the demands of royal life."

"Sounds lovely," she agreed. "But won't you be lonely in such a remote place?"

Her about to be brother-in-law smiled in understanding. "Typical. You romantics can't wait for the rest of the world to pair off."

She reached for Mathiaz's hand. "Can you blame us for wanting you to find your own happiness?"

"I'll be happy enough walking through the rainforest, swimming in the lakes and photographing the wildlife."

Mathiaz laughed. "Spoken like a true romantic. You won't find much love alone in the wilderness."

"Maybe that's the reason I'm keen to go."

He didn't elaborate and Mathiaz didn't press him. Jacinta didn't yet feel close enough to Eduard to ask, so she said instead, "None of us knows where true love will appear." In her case, it had certainly been true. "We'll soon find out if there's someone for you, waiting in the wilderness."

Eduard smiled to take any sting out of his words. "As you Americans say, don't hold your breath."

"I'll remind you of this conversation when I propose the toast to you and *your* bride-to-be," Mathiaz promised.

Eduard stared out into the night and tried not to sound too sour. "I'm afraid you're both in for a long wait."

Did he imagine it, or did he hear a faint reply whispering on the wind, "Not as long as you might think."

He turned to look at his brother and his fiancée but they had melted into one another's arms in the shadows, and were far too preoccupied to have spoken.

Eduard shivered slightly, wondering what he had heard if, indeed, he had heard anything at all. The last few months had been long and demanding. He needed a break, that was all. He certainly didn't begrudge Mathiaz his happiness, and he liked his prospective sister-in-law a lot. But he wasn't looking for love. He was happy enough as he was, he told himself.

Turning discreetly back to face the garden, he couldn't entirely suppress a twinge of envy. He couldn't deny it would be pleasant to have someone to come home to, to share confidences with, and passion of the kind he felt sparking like electricity between Mathiaz and Jacinta. Maybe there would be a baby, too, in time.

Enough, he told himself sternly. He shouldn't let their fond hopes get to him. The sooner he could head for the sanctuary of Tiga Falls Lodge, the better. Jacinta's confident assertion that true love might be waiting for him there was romantic, but impossible.

Wasn't it?

Listening to the wind sighing among the trees, Eduard was no longer so sure.

* * * * *

Is there someone waiting for Eduard?
Find out next month in

THE MARQUIS & THE MOTHER-TO-BE!
(SR #1633)

COMING NEXT MONTH

#1630 THE WOLF'S SURRENDER—Sandra Steffen
The Coltons
Kelly Madison had been the bane of the Honorable Grey Colton's existence. Now the feisty defense attorney was back in town, in his courtroom…and ready to give birth! Grey helped deliver her baby—and, to his surprise, softened toward the single mom. But would his ambitions drive him up the legal ladder—or into Kelly's arms?

#1631 LIONHEARTED—Diana Palmer
Long, Tall Texans
Inexperienced debutante Janie Brewster had been chasing successful rancher Leo Hart for years—but he only saw her as a child. At a friend's suggestion, she set out to prove herself a bona fide cowgirl. But would her rough-and-tumble image be enough to win over a sexy, stubborn Hart?

#1632 GUESS WHO'S COMING FOR CHRISTMAS?—Cara Colter
Beth Cavell promised her orphaned nephew snow for Christmas—then handsome Scrooge Riley Keenan appeared and threatened all her plans. When an unexpected storm forced them to spend the holiday together, Beth wondered if Riley could grant Jamie's other Christmas wish—a new daddy!

#1633 THE MARQUIS AND THE MOTHER-TO-BE—Valerie Parv
The Carramer Legacy
The Marquis of Merrisand might be royalty, but that didn't mean that he could claim Carissa Day's lodge as his own! Except that it *was* his, and Carissa was the victim of a con man. A true gentleman, would Eduard de Marigny open his home—and his heart—to the pregnant temptress?

#1634 THE BILLIONAIRE BORROWS A BRIDE—Myrna Mackenzie
The Wedding Auction
Wanting no part of romance, Spencer Fairfield hired Kate Ryerson to pose as his fiancée—after all, Kate supposedly had a fiancé of her own so there would be no expectations. But his ruse wasn't working the way he'd planned, and soon Spencer discovered the only man Kate did have in her life—was himself!

#1635 THE DOCTOR'S PREGNANT PROPOSAL—Donna Clayton
The Thunder Clan
Devastatingly handsome Grey Thunder wasn't interested in a real marriage—but he *was* interested in a pretend one! Marrying the emotionally scarred doctor was the perfect solution to pregnant Lori Young's problems. But could their tentative yet passionate bond help them face the pain of their pasts?

SRCNM1102